Lord Dunsany
The Blessing of Pan
I0581805

HEATHEN EDITIONS
THEIR BOOKS. OUR WAY.

Published in the good ole United States of America
by Heathen Editions, an imprint of
Heathen Creative
P.O. Box 588
Point Pleasant, WV 25550-0588

Heathen Editions are available at quantity discounts.
Bear witness to the yackety-yak and tomfoolery at:

heatheneditions.com

Social? Tag us! @heatheneditions
Photo? Tag it! #heathenedition

Caution: This book may alter your mind.

First published September 1927
Heathen Edition published September 1, 2025

Paperback ISBN: 978-1-948316-49-1
Hardcover ISBN: 978-1-963228-49-6

Book and cover design by Sheridan Cleland
Set in 11.5pt Crimson Pro
Chapters in Rilley

FIRST HEATHEN EDITION

And what was there
to know of
the Old Stones?
"Come and I'll tell you.
Come and I'll tell you.
Come and I'll tell you,"
sang the strange tune
like chimes . . .

To
S. H. SIME[1]

---

[1] Sidney Herbert Sime (1865–1941), who signed his works S. H. Sime, was an early 20th century English artist, mostly remembered for his fantasy and satirical artwork, especially his story illustrations for Dunsany.

Heathenry
Thoughts on the Text

First, an acknowledgment is in order: while it's plausible that we may have eventually stumbled onto and/or discovered this Dunsany novel and Heathenized it on our own, this particular **Heathen Edition** exists right here, right now because it was requested by one of our readers (fans? adherents? supporters? — I'm still unsure which word is the right word to describe anyone who enjoys and/or collects our books).

How it happened was simple: Juan A. emailed us a list of books for **Heathen** consideration and, after dutiful research, we concluded that, at the very least, ***The Blessing of Pan*** might be a worthwhile endeavor — and here we are — or, as the French say, *et voilà!*

Thanks, Juan! To you, and to all, we hope our rendition exceeds your expectations.

Juan also suggested some other great books. So many great books, in fact, that we wish there were more hours in a day, and more days in a week. But we'll get to them. Eventually. *Maybe!*

Second, let's address the heathen in the room.

If you're unfamiliar with our work and picked this book up thinking its **"Heathen Edition"** label was in some way a promotion or glorification of a godless heathen nature, then here's where we pull the ol' switcheroo ... you see, we're Appalachian God-fearing (capital H) **Heathens**, and as such our take on this pastoral tale is probably a mighty sight different than your typical godless (lowercase h) heathen.

Whereas a heathen may find this book a call for and/or a return to paganism, we **Heathens** see the exact inverse: we view it as a cautionary tale that every Christian should read in order to better, nay wholly (yes, Holy) understand and strengthen their guard against the infectious nature of sin, especially if they're of the ilk who search for God *without* while ignoring the Divine Spark *within*.

But, we're getting ahead of ourselves———

Let's backup and talk Dunsany — a writer whose lineage was noble, whose language was biblical, and whose imagination was mythic — a man who didn't just inherit a castle; he inherited a worldview shaped by Scripture, sunsets, and sylvas.

Born in London on July 24, 1878, Edward John Moreton Drax Plunkett inherited the title of Lord Dunsany — specifically 18th Baron Dunsany — at just 20 years old, following his father's death in 1899.[1]

Of Anglo-Irish descent, he belonged to one of Ireland's oldest noble families, the title Baron of Dunsany being among the most ancient in the Peerage of Ireland,[2] dating back to the 13th century, with the Plunkett name having passed, now, through 21 of its generations. Their ancestral seat, Dunsany Castle in County Meath, built circa 1180, remains one of Ireland's longest continuously inhabited homes — possibly the longest by a single family.

It's also worth noting that Dunsany fought in the Second Boer War and World War I, and while on leave during the latter

---

[1] John William Plunkett, 17th Baron of Dunsany (1853–1899) was an Anglo-Irish Conservative politician.

[2] Titles of nobility created by the English monarchs in their capacity as Lord or King of Ireland, or later by monarchs of the United Kingdom of Great Britain and Ireland, the practice of which came to an end in the 19th century.

heard of disturbances in Dublin during the Easter Rising of 1916 and went to offer assistance and was wounded by a bullet to the skull for his troubles. He was an avid horseman and hunter, becoming at one time the pistol-shooting champion of Ireland, and was also a keen chess player, again becoming a one-time champion of Ireland, and even invented an asymmetrical variant of the game called Dunsany's Chess.

It's tempting to imagine that such a lineage, steeped in adventure, tradition, and centuries of history, might have predisposed Dunsany's literary efforts. Yet what emerged from his pen was not clever reframings of autobiography, but grand myths of his own invention — conjured in the learned, archaic language of his youth.

In the 1917 *Bellman* feature "Lord Dunsany's Peculiar Genius" Montrose J. Moses[3] notes:

> "It is said that when Dunsany was a boy his reading was watched carefully. He was confined mostly to the Bible, to Grimm[4] and Hans Andersen,[5] and to the literature and mythology of Greece. These were his models, and there are some enthusiastic adherents who see in Dunsany's prose the influence of the King James version; who measure his poetic imagination by the direct influence he had from Greek legend."[6]

And in 1922, H.P. Lovecraft[7] wrote:

---

[3] Montrose Jonas Moses (1878–1934) was an American author.

[4] The Brothers Grimm, Jacob (1785–1863) and Wilhelm (1786–1859), were German academics who together collected and published some of the world's best-known folktales.

[5] Hans Christian Andersen (1805–1875) was a Danish author best remembered for his literary fairy tales.

[6] Moses, M.J. (1917, April 14). Lord Dunsany's Peculiar Genius. *The Bellman* 22(561), p. 406.

[7] Howard Phillips Lovecraft (1890–1937) was an American author of weird, horror, fantasy, and science fiction, best known for his creation of the Cthulhu Mythos.

ends p. xxiv

"Dunsany's earliest youth was spent at the ancestral estate of his mother[8] . . . He had a room whose windows faced the hills and the sunset, and to these vistas of golden earth and sky he attributes much of his poetic tendency. His unique manner of expression was promoted by his mother's careful choice of his reading; newspapers were wholly excluded, and the King James Bible made the principal article of literary diet. The effect of this reading on his style was permanent and marvellously beneficial. The simplicity and purity of archaic English, and the artistic repetitions of the Hebrew psalmists, all became his without conscious effort; so that to this day he has escaped the vitiation common to most modern prose writers.

"At his first public school, Cheam School,[9] Dunsany received still more of the biblical influence, and obtained his first touch of an influence still more valuable: that of the Greek classics. In Homer[10] he found a spirit of wonder akin to his own, and throughout his work one may trace the inspiration of the *Odyssey* — an epic, by the way, which . . . teems with just that glamour of strange, far lands which is Dunsany's prime attribute."[11]

Reading Lovecraft's framing of the narrative, one might be inclined to laud the mother for the relegation of her son's formative reading material. However, it isn't until one seeks the source of that information that the truth of the matter is

---

[8] Ernle Elizabeth Louisa Maria Grosvenor Ernle-Erle-Drax (née Burton) (1855–1916).

[9] Founded originally as a boys school in 1645, Cheam School, today, is a mixed preparatory school located in Headley, Hampshire, England.

[10] Homer (c. 8th century BC) was a Greek poet credited as the author of the *Iliad* and the *Odyssey*, two epic poems that are foundational works of ancient Greek literature.

[11] Although first written in 1922, it wasn't published until 1944, in the Lovecraft collection *Marginalia* by Arkham House.

fully understood; in a letter to Irish-American author Frank Harris,[12] Dunsany elaborates:

> "I think I owe most of my style to the reports of proceedings in the divorce court; were it not for these my mother might have allowed me to read newspapers before I went to school; as it was she never did. I began reading Grimm and Andersen. I remember reading them in the evening with twilight coming on. All the windows of rooms I used in the house in Kent where I was brought up faced the sunset . . . When I went to Cheam School I was given a lot of the Bible to read. This turned my thoughts eastward. For years no style seemed to me natural but that of the Bible and I feared that I never would become a writer when I saw that other people did not use it. When I learned Greek at Cheam and heard of other gods a great pity came on me for those beautiful marble people that had become forsaken and this mood has never quite left me."

In that single paragraph we believe you get the whole of the engine that propelled Dunsany's literary efforts because you glean the biblical sway, you glimpse the genesis of mythical affinity, and the long-term influence of his parents' separation should most assuredly never be understated.

Our research uncovered little information regarding their separation, which is unsurprising when one considers the formalities and discretion of aristocratic families of the time. Even the UK Parliament website currently states: "Before 1914 divorce was rare; it was considered a scandal, confined by expense to the rich." So, we are only aware of what Dunsany stated in that letter to Harris, plus a tidbit from his father's Wiki — "His widow, Ernle, from whom he was separated in his last years," — and we also know that Cheam School is for

---

[12] Frank Harris (1856–1931) was an Irish-American editor, novelist, short story writer, journalist, and publisher.

ends p. xxiv

children up to age 13. And with a bit of math — parents married 1877, Dunsany born 1878, father died 1899 — we can assume his parents separated sometime around 1890-ish. Which is to say that they separated during important formative years of Dunsany's childhood.

The English are well-known for their mannerly restraint, which makes us curious if the "great pity" Dunsany expressed for those Greek statues was in reality an outlet for repressed and unprocessed emotions from his parents' separation?

Also curious is that even in spite of the strong adolescent biblical influence, noted weird fiction scholar S.T. Joshi[13] reveals:

> "Lord Dunsany, although raised as a Protestant, was in all likelihood an atheist … Although by no means being the dogged opponent of religious belief that his disciple H. P. Lovecraft was, Dunsany ultimately seems to have come to the conclusion that conventional Christianity was in league with the forces of modernism."[14]

E. F. Bleiler[15] also tells us:

> "*The Blessing of Pan* is vintage Dunsany, expressing in musical language his love of uncontaminated nature, his hatred of modern business and technology, his contempt for Christianity, and his fondness for forgotten gods. 'I am sad, master, when the old gods go,' remarks a servant in Dunsany's play *If* (1922). 'But they are bad

---

[13] Sunand Tryambak Joshi (1958–) is an American literary critic whose work has largely focused on weird and fantastic fiction, especially the life and work of H. P. Lovecraft.

[14] Joshi, S.T. (2013). Christianity and Paganism in Two Dunsany Novels. *Critical Essays on Lord Dunsany* (p. 203). The Scarecrow Press.

[15] Everett Franklin Bleiler (1920–2010) was an American editor, bibliographer, and scholar of science fiction, detective fiction, and fantasy literature.

gods, Daoud,' says his master. Daoud replies, 'I am sad when the bad gods go.'"[16]

Perhaps Dunsany's "fondness for forgotten gods," even the bad ones, was simply a manifestation of memories and a longing for happier times of his youth? Perhaps mythopoeia[17] became the avenue of that expression? Our hunch is reinforced by a brief passing note from Patrick Maume:[18]

"He spent his childhood at his mother's home, Dunstall Priory in Shoreham, in Southeast Kent. Dunsany's education intensified his sense of his Kent childhood as a lost paradise."[19]

In his first autobiography, *Patches of Sunlight*, Dunsany himself ventures a guess as to a *why* when he tells of a teacher who "took an enormous amount of trouble to hammer Greek into me, and very nearly made me a Greek scholar," but then young Dunsany was sent to a crammer's[20] from Eton[21] and missed out on further Greek teachings that:

" . . . left me with a curious longing for the mighty lore of the Greeks, of which I had had glimpses like a child seeing wonderful flowers through the shut gates of a garden; and it may have been the retirement of the Greek

---

[16] Bleiler, E. F. (1985). Lord Dunsany. *Supernatural Fiction Writers: Fantasy and Horror*, Vol. 1 (p. 474). Charles Scribner's Sons.

[17] The making of a myth or myths.

[18] A researcher with the Royal Irish Academy's Dictionary of Irish Biography, who has published extensively on nineteenth- and twentieth-century Irish history.

[19] Maume, P. (2009). Dreams of Empire, Empire of Dreams: Lord Dunsany Plays the Game. *New Hibernia Review* 13(4), p. 14.

[20] A British term that means: a person or institution that prepares students for an examination intensively over a short period of time.

[21] Established in 1440, Eton College is a public school providing boarding education for boys aged 13–18, in the small town of Eton, Berkshire, England.

ends p. xxiv

gods from my vision after I left Eton that eventually drove me to satisfy some such longing by making gods unto myself, as I did in my first two books."[22]

Perchance, has anyone ever accused Dunsany of being a sentimentalist? It's plausible, too, that we're reading far too much into all of this, as Montrose Moses relays in the afore-mentioned *Bellman* feature:

> "People are forever reading in Dunsany what he does not wish them to read. In his correspondence, he declares: 'When I write of Babylon there are people who cannot see that I write of it for love of Babylon's ways, and they think I'm thinking of London still and our beastly Parliament.'"[23]

What's certain, though, is that Dunsany, as Bleiler noted, had contempt for Christianity, and whereas Joshi seems unsure of Dunsany's atheism, Maume leaves no doubt:

> "Dunsany was an atheist, though attentive to Anglican observances in later life. His writings imply that he believed most contemporary British Christians were well-meaning naifs ignorant of the harsh Oriental world where their religion began."[24]

What we don't know, and what we can't seem to locate in any literature, is the exact reason for that atheism. Which would be a wondrous bit of biography to possess when analyzing a story of Parson versus Pan, which brings us back to the cautionary tale (as we view it) that is ***The Blessing of Pan***.

---

[22] The Book of Earth. (1938). *Patches of Sunlight* (p. 30). William Heinemann Ltd.

[23] Moses, M.J. (1917, April 14). Lord Dunsany's Peculiar Genius. *The Bellman* 22(561), p. 407.

[24] Maume, P. (2009). Dreams of Empire, Empire of Dreams: Lord Dunsany Plays the Game. *New Hibernia Review* 13(4), p. 21.

With that, we issue two warnings:
1. Spoilers ahead!
2. It may be more beneficial to:
   A. Read the story, first, then return here to read our analysis, or:
   B. Skip our following analysis entirely and go enjoy the story. Indeed, Dunsany would probably agree:

"But in case I shall not be able to explain my work, I think the first thing to tell them [the public] is that it does not need explanation. One does not explain a sunset, nor does one need to explain a work of art. One may analyze, of course; that is profitable and interesting, but the growing demand to be told What It's All About before one can even enjoy becomes absurd."[25]

Continuing on, and before we return to his atheism, let's examine what Dunsany himself had to say about his *Blessing*.

In his second autobiography, *While the Sirens Slept*, Dunsany states:

"On 19th August [1926] I started again on that very laborious undertaking, writing a novel. An idea had suddenly come to me; and, when I sat down to write, it easily worked itself out. That is to say the story unrolled itself without any difficulty, but the labour of writing seventy thousand words is not easy, and that is the length that a novel has to be. It may be longer, but God forbid that I should take longer than that to tell a story. This book was called *The Blessing of Pan*, and told how the whole of an English village came gradually under Pan's influence, while a clergy man fought the influence alone, unaided by Authority; because Authority preferred to take the

[25] Moses, M.J. (1917, April 14). Lord Dunsany's Peculiar Genius. *The Bellman* 22(561), p. 409.

ends p. xxiv

line of refusing to recognize that such a dreadful state of things could be. So in the end Pan wins."[26]

Then, after a bit of digression, he returns to its conclusion five paragraphs later:

"Meanwhile from the neighbouring shore of the world of dreams I was still digging my **Blessing of Pan**, but slowly, for I had only worked four days in October, four in November, two in December and none at all in January. But as the shooting season ended, and a month later the hunting season, I worked harder and the book was finished in Kent, whence the idea had come, on 12th May, 1927."[27]

Our research reveals that the book was published in the U.K. during the last week of September 1927.

And, doubling back for a moment, to further augment our hunch of Dunsany channeling his childhood, we would certainly be remiss if we did not bring your attention to this Pan-centric admission from *Patches of Sunshine*:

"On the back of the hill that faced Dunstall, the slope of which I could now see facing West from the end of Sir Joseph's[28] garden, I first saw a hare one summer's evening: my father pointed him out to me and clapped his hands for me to see it run; and it ran along the slope under the woods. If ever I have written of Pan, out in the evening, as though I had really seen him, it is mostly a memory of that hare. If I thought that I was a gifted individual whose inspirations came sheer from outside earth

---

[26] In Happy Isles. (1944). *While the Sirens Slept* (p. 85). Jarrolds London Ltd.

[27] Ibid. p. 86

[28] Joseph Prestwich (1812–1896) was a British geologist and businessman, known as an expert on the Tertiary Period and for having confirmed the findings of ancient flint tools in the Somme valley gravel beds.

and transcended common things, I should not write this book; but I believe that the wildest flights of the fancies of any of us have their homes with Mother Earth, and I only retail my early memories because amongst them must be the origins of any fancies of mine that may have been so happy as to entertain any reader."[29]

Now, returning to Dunsany's atheism: since we don't know the exact reason for it the only thing we can do is glean reasoning from his writing, and his treatment and rendering of the Anglican Church and its parishioners is telling.

The first thing one well-versed in Christian teachings may notice upon finishing the book is that at no time during the story does Reverend Anwrel ever pray to God, or call on Him for Holy instruction.

Anwrel is seemingly always searching for Divine assistance *outside* of himself. First, by notifying, in writing, then visiting, in person, his bishop, then meeting with another local priest and Greek scholar, Hetley, before abandoning his Holy institution altogether and seeking guidance from the local shamanistic madman Perkin.

In fact, the only time Anwrel does pray in the entire story is when he prays for Perkin's arrival.[30] Not that it matters, for the best advice Perkin can ever offer is, "Keep your illusions, man; keep your illusions,"[31] which should probably be read in a curt English tone, yet we can't help but hear it à la 1970s Dennis Hopper: "Keep your illusions, *maaaaan.*" And that is in no way pejorative! For our money, Perkin is the best character in the book, and we were quite pleased to discover that Dunsany thought the same:

"A queer old character walked right into this book, as

---

[29] Dunstall. (1938). *Patches of Sunlight* (p. 9). William Heinemann Ltd.
[30] See p. 144
[31] See p. 122

ends p. xxiv

I was writing it, as though of his own accord, and was I think the best character in it."[32]

When even Perkin's advice doesn't help, Anwrel's desperate all-for-naught outsourcing of spiritual responsibility culminates when he vainly attempts to prepare a sermon:

He had his Bible before him and all his books of reference, and his white sheet of foolscap and the red and black ink-pots; but not a word would come. He sat there for an hour, and still the paper was blank. Still he sat on. It is seldom that a man tries as Anwrel was trying now, and finds that nothing comes as the fruit of such intensity. Yet nothing came to Anwrel . . . He needed instances, whether in the Bible itself, or in the writings of the early fathers, or in some modern work of learned ecclesiastics, that should confound this heresy; and then he required to prove, for it was of no use merely quoting, that these great authorities were indubitably right. But no such instance could he find upon which to build his argument. Nothing on which even to begin the long proof that should convince the minds of his people that they had been doing utterly wrong; without which convincing he knew now that they would go so far astray, that when the scandal spread to the ears of those that should have helped him, it would be all too late. He read and he reasoned. But when he left his study late that evening, worn with the strain of work, the sheet of foolscap was still untouched on his desk. He had not even found a text.[33]

This isn't just about the encroachment of paganism, it's about the hollowing out of institutional faith, and the quiet

---

[32] In Happy Isles. (1944). *While the Sirens Slept* (p. 85). Jarrolds London Ltd.
[33] See p. 153

unraveling of a man who no longer knows how to commune with the Divine. Anwrel is not a shepherd guiding his flock, he's a functionary trying to sustain a crumbling institution, and, ultimately, a symbol of supreme spiritual disconnection. He performs the rituals, clings to the structure, reads the texts, but never seeks direct communion with God.

It's as if he has forgotten that such a connection is possible, if he even knew it was possible to begin with.

In Luke 17, when the Pharisees demand that Jesus tell them when the kingdom of God should come, He answers:

> "The kingdom of God cometh not with observation: Neither shall they say, Lo here! or, lo there! for, behold, the kingdom of God is within you."

Anwrel always seeks *without* for authority, for validation, for rescue, but never *within*, never toward the indwelling presence of the Divine. He solicits help from *without*, from the bishop, from Hetley, from Perkin, but never *within* from God. That is, in part, what makes the novel so haunting: it's less a story of good vs. evil and more a meditation on spiritual entropy, wherein, through the perception of our pastoral protagonist, a pagan god appears more "alive" than the Christian one. Anwrel fails not because he faces temptation, but because he has no spiritual depth to resist "the very pipes of Pan." His spiritual life is performative, not participatory. His tragedy is not that he loses his parish, it's that he never truly possessed the faith he preached. The absence of prayer isn't just a narrative omission; it's a theological void. He is a priest who lacks wholly (yes, Holy) Divine communion.

Pan's music, in this light, becomes a metaphor for sacrilegious seduction — not just of the body, but of a soul untethered from its source. The villagers succumb because they are attracted by something vital and ecstatic, but Anwrel succumbs because he has no defense. He is not tempted *away* from God, he is tempted *in the absence* of God. The music of Pan's pipes fill the silence where prayer should have been.

In Chapter 28, Anwrel questions why Pan chose Wolding:

> "But why, why did he come here?" cried Anwrel . . . And still his mind was full of all the other places he might have gone to, with his sly pretence of being a clergyman. Why not to one of them instead of Wolding? Such thoughts are common to all troubles . . . But still he uttered the cry of all minds that first come on a trouble: "Why here?"[34]

The answer, Anwrel, old chap, is that in Warfare 101 the enemy is taught to attack where there is the *least* resistance.

Cue Revelation 3:16, which states:

> "So then because thou art lukewarm, and neither cold nor hot, I will spue thee out of my mouth."

Once you become aware of it, Anwrel's spiritual tepidity is almost painful to witness. He's not a heretic, nor a zealot — he's a man who drifts, who goes through the motions of faith without Holy conviction or Divine intimacy. Dunsany doesn't need to show Anwrel sinning in a conventional sense; his lukewarmness *is* the sin. It's what makes him vulnerable to Pan's seduction — not because he's tempted by pleasure, but because he's spiritually unmoored. Said another way, he is not Holy anchored to the Rock, which brings us to Matthew 7:24-27:

> "Therefore whosoever heareth these sayings of mine, and doeth them, I will liken him unto a wise man, which built his house upon a rock: And the rain descended, and the floods came, and the winds blew, and beat upon that

---

[34] See pp. 150-151

house; and it fell not: for it was founded upon a rock. And every one that heareth these sayings of mine, and doeth them not, shall be likened unto a foolish man, which built his house upon the sand: And the rain descended, and the floods came, and the winds blew, and beat upon that house; and it fell: and great was the fall of it."

These verses soar near allegory when applied to Anwrel. His "house" — his ministry, his theology, his identity — is built on institutional scaffolding, not on the Rock of Christ. He relies on the authority of the diocese, the structure of the church, and all the *appearances* of holiness — but when the "rain descends," when Pan's influence spreads and the villagers depart, one by one, his foundation crumbles. He has no inner fortress, no spiritual architecture to withstand the storm. His surrender to paganism is not a conversion, it's the collapse of his (lowercase h) holy house of cards which he built upon the sand.

It's almost as if, rather than glorifying paganism, Dunsany uses this narrative as an X-ray to expose the weakness of unrooted faith; as if Dunsany isn't a pagan fantasist, but, by channeling the quiet horror of Divine absence, becomes an inadvertent chronicler of metaphysical capitulation. Pan is not the villain — he's the test. And Anwrel fails not because Pan is powerful, but because Anwrel is spiritually vacant.

In that way, we see **The Blessing of Pan** not as a celebration of pagan resurgence, but as spiritual tragedy, a cautionary tale about the dangers of externalizing the search for God and His assistance, of mistaking liturgical ritual for Holy relationship, and of forsaking the Divine Spark *within*.

And now, here we are, and we still don't know why Dunsany was an atheist.

What we find surprising about this particular allegation is that in the whole of Dunsany's currently known bibliography — which spans 90 books, hundreds of short stories, and plays, and essays — nowhere does Dunsany himself state *outright* that he is an atheist, which, in our experience, is so *unlike* an atheist.

ends p. xxiv

Indeed, in our experience, atheists usually have no problem whatsoever telling you *exactly why* they identify as such, and if a soapbox isn't readily available, then any ole box will do.

The same goes for many (some, not all) agnostics, too.

It would seem, based on our research, that this atheist label that so many literary critics want to gleefully hang on Dunsany is *interpretively* inferred from his writings and not *actually* sourced directly from the horse's mouth, as they say.

Sure, we can be dogmatically journalistic about it and provide you with two sources that claim Dunsany was an atheist, then happily claim he's an atheist, too, and party on. And if two sources aren't enough, then how about, say, fifty?

The problem is that they're all just that: *claims.*

> **claim** *noun*
> an assertion of the truth of something, typically
> one that is disputed or in doubt

During our research, one of the examples that we've seen utilized more than once to cement Dunsany's atheist status is drawn from one of his early plays, *The Glittering Gate*,[35] wherein two criminals break into Heaven only to find a vast emptiness.

We are reminded: *Lo here! Lo there!*

And *lo!* if interpretation is the name of the game, well, then, re: Appalachian — *takes sip* — hold our beer, watch this:

Dunsany was **not** an atheist.

Agnostic? *Maybe.*

Pantheist? *Maybe*, and by extension:

Omnist? *Maybe.*

But atheist? *Absolutely not.*

Skeptic of organized religion? *Without a doubt.*

For our money, Perkin is the key to understanding Dunsany's religious views . . .

---

[35] Collected in his 1914 book *Five Plays.*

Once again *and* straight from the horse's mouth:

> "A queer old character walked right into this book, as I was writing it, as though of his own accord, and was I think the best character in it."

He's the "best character" because his warning — "Keep your illusions, man; keep your illusions" — is the closest thing to divine insight in the novel; it's not a sneer but a benediction. That line suggests that illusion may be all that's left — that belief, whether Christian or pagan, is a fragile construct we cling to in the face of cosmic indifference.

And yet, Perkin's madness is not chaos — it's clarity. He sees through Anwrel's spiritual collapse, and his advice is both ironic and compassionate. In a world where Pan is rising and the old gods stir, where paganism regenerates as Anwrel's church crumbles, the only salvation may lie in preserving the *illusion* of meaning — and Perkin alone sees that truth: that belief, whether liturgical or mythical, may be nothing more than a veil against the void . . .

> "I lost my illusions."
> "Lost your illusions?" said Anwrel.
> "Yes."
> "How did that happen?"
> "I'll tell you. I saw the mayor in all his robes one day. I just laughed at it all. I saw tall silk hats and laughed again: I do to this day. And I saw the cathedral with its coloured windows, and I laughed at that too. The illusion went out of everything. That's how it happened."
>
>   . . .
>
> "Are you much troubled?" asked Anwrel.
> "Yes," said the man. "You see my illusions are gone. They're the only defence we have."[36]

---

[36] See p. 121

ends next p.

Dunsany may have written Anwrel's downfall as a lament for hollow religion — but in Perkin, he gives voice to something deeper. It is no accident that Dunsany called him "the best character in it," for Perkin mirrors Dunsany's own spiritual outlook — not in Anwrel's waning orthodoxy, nor in the villagers' pagan ecstasy, but in the quiet resignation that meaning must be invented, preserved, and clung to, even as the gods — old or new — gaze on with insouciance.

Dunsany, like Perkin, likely viewed all spiritual experiences, Christian *and* pagan, as illusions. And if he believed, like Perkin, that religious experiences are powerful but illusory, then this may explain why he didn't outright subscribe to any one label, religious or irreligious, seeing them as irrelevant and unnecessary to the creation of his own stories and myths.

But, we imagine that *if* Dunsany *had* to choose, then Perkin's fate serves as testament: "Perkin stayed on, and never left Wolding again."[37]

We can hear Hopper yet:

Keep your illusions wholly (yes, Holy), *maaaaan.*

But, for we **Heathens**, in sum: seek the Rock, not the ritual.

Finally, as for the text, seeing as how this a very British story, both in its setting and its telling, we've retained Dunsany's wistful, whimsical British English. Our only modifications have been in streamlining several hyphened words so they read a bit easier for modern eyes: week-day is now weekday, folk-lore has become folklore, and so on.

The true bulk of our work lies in the nearly 200 footnotes that we've appended to enhance your reading, as well as to provide clarity, context, and commentary where necessary.

In all, we think our edition is . . .

We think our . . .

We . . .

Do you hear that?

It sounds like———

---

[37] See p. 193

1

The Vicar of Wolding[1]

A blowfly[2] poised upon the summer air, that had burned the may[3] but scarce brought out the rose, was maintaining his perfect stillness by a whirl of wingbeats too swift for a brain to calculate or even an eye to see: the small clear body hung between two blurs caused by his wingbeats, above a lawn underneath beech trees: and a clergyman, plump and touched with grey, such a one as seemed just to have entered the placid years with the sharper cares left behind him, was watching the blowfly from out of a long wicker chair. The dark-clad form lying back in the wicker chair suggested an immobility as complete as the one that the blowfly only achieved by such a whirl of wings, but under the quiet face troubled thoughts were well astir. Then the blowfly with a dart of incredible suddenness went sidelong away to poise himself motionless elsewhere, but the man in the chair remained with the same thoughts.

[1] Wolding is a village of Dunsany's invention, it does not exist.

[2] A large metallic blue, green, or black-bodied fly that deposits its eggs in carcasses or in open sores and wounds.

[3] The blossom of a hawthorn (a thorny shrub or tree of the rose family, with white, pink, or red blossoms and haws, which are its small dark red fruits).

The vicar had been troubled for several days, at first by uncertainty almost amounting to fear, then, when the facts were certain, by wondering what he should do, and then, when he knew what he ought to do, by evasions and mere postponements; he was in a treadmill of thought that went uselessly round and round to the same point: he ought to write to the Bishop. Having seen that, there was no more to think about than "What will the Bishop think?"; "Will he be at the Palace on Tuesday?"; "Will he get it any sooner if I write before tomorrow, on account of the Sunday post?" And the insects changed in the still glittering air, those of the midday giving place to such as haunted the evening, and the light began to beat up under the beech-leaves, and it was coming near to the time when that strange tune would be heard again from the hill, piercing the air like a moonbeam, and thrilling the gloaming[4] with that sheer touch of magic that he knew it was right to dread.

And that day he tarried no longer, but rose all at once from his chair and went indoors, and into the little room that was called his study, and took pen and paper at once. His wife saw him come in, and said some idle word to him, but did nothing that would delay him, for she saw by a look on his face that all the trouble of the last few days, of which he said never a word to her, was now at some kind of climax. He wrote hurriedly: the difficulty was in beginning the letter at all, not in how to word it; he was sure of his facts, so far as these were knowable, and his mind was full of phrases that he had turned over and over for nearly a week, he had only to pour them out. By the opening and shutting of doors and familiar clickings he heard the tea-things being brought in late, but no one disturbed him there writing alone. And this was the letter that he wrote the Bishop:

Wolding Vicarage, Seldham,
Wealdborough,
June 10th.

---

[4] Twilight or dusk.

My Lord,

In my great perplexity I am impelled to encroach upon your Lordship's time to ask advice and guidance. And before I write down the facts just as they are known to me I will ask your Lordship to bear in mind that Wolding has never been an ordinary parish this sixteen or seventeen years, and is not yet, and that — do what I can — I have been unable to eliminate queer tales that, were they older, might be called folklore, and a queer point of view, and, even where I am able to partially suppress these, queer memories among the older people. In fact, although I cannot lay a finger on anything definite he did that was wrong, Wolding suffered irreparable injury from the brief stay of the man that called himself the Reverend Arthur Davidson. I know he was ordained before your Lordship's time, and that it is not for me to find any fault with those that sent him here. I merely state as a fact the great difficulties attending all spiritual work in Wolding since he disappeared, and that these difficulties, however intangible, still persist after all this lapse of time, and I ask that they may be borne in mind.

And now, my lord, the facts are these. As soon as the sun is set, or a little sooner, for it is obscured from us early by Wold Hill, there comes the sound of music from the end of the hill, which is some way left of the sunset (at this time of year). It is a flute-like music, and a definite tune, but not a tune known to anyone here, nor one I am able to trace. It has been playing on most evenings all through Spring, and every day this June. I think I first heard some notes of it late one evening last winter, but now there can be no mistaking it. And sometimes I hear it by moonlight. It seems to come from this side of the woods on the top, either just from the shadow of them, or out of some wild-rose bushes there are on the slope. Later it seems to go over the hill, further and further away. At first I thought it was some young man signalling with this very strange tune to some girl in the village. But it is not that, for I went to see. It is no ordinary couple straying away through the wood. I went to the hill-slope one evening. I heard the notes piercingly clear, but could not see the player. And then I saw two or three girls together going up a little path, a kind of track that leads away from the village and goes over Wold Hill. I stayed where I was and the music played again. And then I saw more young girls. Some were going up the path and some were slanting away from it up the wild slope of the hill. All were going toward that music. Then I saw three or four that I knew coming through the briars toward me away from the path, near enough for me to recognise. When they saw me they turned deliberately back to the path, and when they came to it they went on up the hill, toward the woods, away from the village. I do not know how to express it, but they turned at once, as soon as they saw me, almost as wild things might, and went deliberately away to the woods. I desired to state my facts as amply as possible, though fearing that I should encroach too much on your lordship's time; but now that I have stated them I would there were more, for they seem too slight to account for my great perplexity. I can only add that this has happened often. But oh, my lord, believe me when I say that that tune is no common melody, but is something I never have known to come out of music, and has some power I never dreamed to be possible, and I need your help in this trouble as I never needed it yet.

> Your Lordship's obedient servant,
> Elderick Anwrel.

Then he went to the next room to find his wife. And the tea-things were all still here, though the buttered buns were cold.

"The tea's too strong now, dear," she said. "Besides, it's all cold. I'll ring for Marion."

"No, no," he said. Neither sight nor thought of tea had entered his mind. "I have been much perplexed lately. That tune one hears at sunset. I can't make it out at all. I couldn't make it out. So I wrote to the Bishop."

She took the letter thoughtfully and looked at it. Yes, it was as he had said, a letter to the Bishop.

"The tune," she said, "is played by young Tommy Duffin. He plays it on that instrument he made out of bulrushes[5] or some such reeds."

"Tommy Duffin," her husband replied. "They said it was him in the village. Now how would Tommy Duffin have come by any such tune?"

But she was reading the letter attentively and said no more. For a moment she held it in silence when she had finished.

Then she said, "You split the infinitive, dear, where you said 'to partially suppress'."

"Does that matter?" he asked.

"Well, no," she said, "not really. But the Bishop might not like it."

He went back to the study and made the alteration, as tidily as such changes can be made, and then he sat there brooding over the letter. And the more he brooded the more he began to see that he was about to trouble the Bishop needlessly: that whether the tune, which was undoubtedly played, was played by Tommy Duffin, the seventeen-year-old boy whom he remembered christening as one of his earliest duties in that parish, or whether by any other, and whatever interest some silly girls might take in it, the subject of his letter was in any case trivial and would seem far more so if rashly sent to the Palace. No, that was no sensible way to set his mind at ease. And yet his wife agreed with him. She had said little enough, but she would never have let him send that letter to the Bishop unless she had fully agreed with it. There *was* something strange in that tune, whoever played it. But with that letter

[5] Another name for cattails.

lying before him the enormity of troubling the Bishop seemed the more immediate, and all his old perplexities began again. And Marion came in with her trim white apron, turning his mind yet more toward conventional things.

"Will there be any more letters for the post, sir?" she said.

"No, Marion," he said. "No, thank you."

And away she went to the village with a note for the grocer, and a letter to the draper in Seldham,[6] and one of her own to her young man away in Yorkshire.[7]

And then with a colour burning wild in the sky, and a dimness growing on earth, and a touch of cold, the sun went under Wold Hill, and there slipped down the shimmering air from the high hill over the valley, a clear wild tune so remote from the thoughts of man that it seemed to drift down from ages and out of lands with which none of our race has ever had any concern. More elfin than the blackbird, more magical than all nightingales, it thrilled the clergyman's heart with awful longings, which he could no more tell of in words than he could have put words to that tune. It gripped him, it held him there. To say he stood spellbound is not to describe his stillness: he did not even breathe. And all his thoughts, all his emotions, his very consciousness, seemed carried away to far valleys, perhaps not even of earth.

All in an instant the music ceased and the silence came back to the gloaming, and back like a slowly returning tide came the thoughts of every day. The vicar dashed to an envelope; he hastily addressed it to the Bishop Wealdenstone, The Palace, Snichester;[8] he thrust the letter in, and picked up his soft black hat and ran downhill to the Post Office.

---

[6] Another village of Dunsany's invention.

[7] An area of Northern England which was historically a county, named after its county town, the city of York.

[8] Yet another invented village by Dunsany.

2

The Small Talk of Mrs. Duffin

"I posted the letter to the Bishop, Augusta."

"Oh, yes," she said.

There are reasons for names like that: some gorgeous relative of other days, some splendid fancy crossing the mind of a parent, some imperious[1] look perhaps, long ago, on the face of the child herself; there are always reasons. And so this plump elderly good soul had come by the name of Augusta. No one knew why.

They said no more about the letter that day, or about the strange cause of it. She saw that the vicar was a little calmer; and she did not wish, even with a word, to stir again the ripples of his perplexities. But much unprofitable time he spent as the next few days went by, wondering what the Bishop would answer. He knew the Bishop was a man of the world, and trusted him to see far more shrewdly into this mystery than he could ever hope to himself, and yet could not quell his troubled speculations as to what the Bishop would say. And amongst the long working hours of the mind of a man ill at ease

---

[1] Overbearing; domineering.

he found ample time to calculate the ramblings of his letter from town to town, until it would come to Snichester on the morning of the day after, and the Bishop's immediate reply and its arrival at Wolding next morning, the third day from then. In these calculations he was right.

Next morning things seemed brighter to the vicar. The sending of the letter had certainly lifted a load, and the actual sunlight was streaming into the house so that some of the breakfast things dazzled.

"I think of going to see Duffin," said the vicar.

"There wouldn't be much to be got from him," his wife answered.

"Have you spoken to him about it?" he asked.

"Not directly," she said.

"No, of course Duffin isn't the sort of man," said the vicar, "that would understand very much about anything like that. But I can ask him. I can ask him where that boy of his goes of an evening."

"Oh, it's him all right," she said.

"It's odd," he said. "The Duffins."

And very soon after breakfast he took his hat and his ash-plant[2] and went to the farm in the valley, beyond the village, where Duffin lived, and had lived all his life. He passed down a little lane with may on one side, across which the seasons went to wake the wild rose on the other; past Duffin's dog in a barrel; across a track trampled to mud by cows morning and evening; and up to the porch of the old farmhouse through a few yards of rose-garden. He found the bell-handle amongst a mass of honeysuckle that was not yet in bloom: he pulled out a rusty length of it, the noise of it grating through the house long before a bell at the back began to wake to an unaccustomed tinkle; and there was Duffin at the door in his shirtsleeves.

"Good morning, Duffin," said the vicar.

"*Good* morning, sir," said the farmer.

---

[2] *Fraxinus*; a genus of plants in the olive and lilac family.

"I came to ask you if you could let me have some of those eggs again."

"Certainly, sir. Certainly," said Duffin. "Come in."

The vicar entered the hall.

"Some of those brown ones, you know," he said.

"Certainly, sir. They're not laying so well now as they were, those Orpingtons.[3] About how many, sir?"

"Oh; say half a dozen."

"Not more than that? I could let you have two dozen."

They were in the parlour now, the vicar sitting on a very black horsehair sofa. He did not want more than six eggs, because he did not want *any*. Six could always be disposed of, but more might be a nuisance.

"No, I think six will do me nicely."

"I could easily let you have two dozen, sir."

"No, thank you; not today. Another time I might be glad of them."

"Well, I'll get them for you now," said Duffin.

"Thank you so much."

And Duffin went out. From voices and sounds at the back the vicar gathered that Mrs. Duffin was washing, and had been told of his visit, and would go and tidy herself and appear later.

He had not asked the price of the eggs: he knew there was something he had forgotten. He waited a long time.

And then Duffin returned with six brown eggs in a basket.

"You'll let me have the basket back some time, won't you, sir? It's Mrs. Duffin's. She uses it gardening."

"Oh, certainly," said the vicar.

"Thank you, sir," said Duffin.

"By the way," said the vicar, "what's your boy doing now? Were you able to find a job for him?"

"Just helping on the farm, sir."

"Ah, helping on the farm."

---

[3] A British breed of chickens, bred in the late nineteenth century by William Cook of Orpington, a town in Greater London.

ch. ends p. 12

"Helping with the cows and all that. And of course when it comes to hay-time . . ."

"Ah, yes, of course."

"That's what he's doing, sir."

"Yes," said the vicar, "keeps him pretty busy I suppose?"

"Well, you know what boys are, sir."

"Yes, yes, of course." And somehow the vicar did not seem any nearer; when the ruddy farmer came all at once to the point that the vicar was driving at.

"Loafs away in the evening as a rule. Mustn't do that when it comes to hay-making."

"No, certainly not," said the vicar, "you'll see that he doesn't, of course."

"Far as I can, sir."

"You don't find it so easy, of course, to control them at that age."

"Not nowadays, sir," said Duffin.

"Perhaps if you just keep him in now from, say, sunset, you'd have him trained to it, as it were, by the time you want him for hay-making."

"It's not what it used to be, sir," said the farmer, "and it's no use us pretending it is. There's a lot of new ideas going about. A lot of them. Now my old father that had this farm before me, if he saw us doing anything he didn't like, he usen't to say anything; he didn't more than just look; just looked at us, sitting in that old wood chair of his; and if that wasn't enough he'd just crack his whip, that was always hanging near him on the wall, the one he took foxhunting; and that would always be enough, and we'd just stop whatever it was we were doing, whenever we heard that. But now . . ."

"Yes, in some respects," said the vicar, "of course those days were the best."

"In every respect, sir," said the farmer.

"And you find you can't keep young Tommy in of an evening?" said the vicar hurriedly, for in another moment his host would have been talking about the price of corn.

"No, sir, I can't," said he. "To put it straight, I can't. He's off to the hills."

"And what does he do there?" asked the vicar.

But the direct question got him no nearer, and all the answer he got was: "Don't ask me, sir, what they do nowadays. They're beyond me altogether."

And the vicar saw he had no more information to give, so he rose to go, in the hopes of getting away before Mrs. Duffin should come in all tidy. In this he failed for he had barely picked up his eggs before she entered in sequins, or so her black dress and jet brooch appeared to him, looking back on it. And with her came Tommy Duffin, with his hair intensely parted.

"Dumpling the son of suet,"[4] said the vicar to himself, whose mind now and then was astonished by the unclerical thoughts that at moments would pass across it. But Tommy's cheeks looked so red, and his face so fat and vacant, and his hair so brilliantly greasy, that the thought came all by itself.

"I came about some more of your excellent eggs," said the vicar after they had shaken hands.

"Glad, I'm sure," said Mrs. Duffin.

"I'm afraid I interfered with your morning's work," he said.

"Not at all," she answered. It was before the days of 'quite all right.'

"I was just taking them back with me," he said.

But that could not be yet. For Mrs. Duffin enquired after Mrs. Anwrel, and this was followed by small talk, kindly but tiny, wearing the morning away; and all the while Tommy sat in his tidy clothes, looking perfectly vacant.

"I christened him, you know," said the vicar.

"Oh yes," replied Mrs. Duffin. "And we was married the year before you came. Less than a year, really." And there followed more reminiscences. And at last the vicar was able to say his farewells, and just as he picked up the basket he remembered

---

[4] Suet is the raw, white, hard fat of beef, lamb, or mutton found around the loins and kidneys, used for tallow and to make foods including puddings, pastry, and mincemeat.

ch. ends next p.

that it had to be returned, and made a plan all of a sudden. How if he brought it back himself one day a little before sunset, and stayed a bit while Mrs. Duffin talked, and watched the, boy as the light was fading away?

$$3$$

A Sight of the Pipes

"I've just been talking to the Duffins," said the vicar to Mrs. Anwrel. "Young Tommy, doesn't seem to be the boy to be doing that sort of thing."

"It never is the likely ones," she answered "that do those unlikely things."

"That's so," said the vicar, thinking of things that had happened one time and another in the parish.

And that day passed over the vicarage, and over the sunny valley. But, for all the quiet of the little house and its lawns, thoughts were racing through Anwrel's mind in the unprofitable pursuit of the course that the Bishop would take, and how he would deal with this thing that was perturbing the parish of Wolding, even how he would word his letter.

That day he did not return to Duffin's house with the basket, feeling it to be barely a sufficient excuse for two visits on the same day. Instead he sat in a chair outside his house toward evening and watched Wold Hill with a look of strained anxiety. And amongst all the sounds that welled up through the dim gold air beneath the enchantment of evening, nothing reached Anwrel's ears that was not assuredly earthly; sounds only of human cries came up from the valley, faint murmurs of human speech, far ripples of human laughter; and such sounds as the barking of dogs, sheep bleating, a rooster crowing, which are a sort of palisade that man has set up between his homes and the silences of the stars. It was not every evening that the tune called from the hill, and Anwrel felt certain that for this silence it was all the more sure to be heard on the following evening.

Next day he was anxious and silent all the morning. He was not by profession a fighting man, yet he was going nearer, and of his own free will, to a power he felt to be awful; and even if it were not Tommy Duffin that played the tune that so haunted the evening, yet he knew that by going down to the farm in the valley he would be far nearer to Wold Hill, and at the hour he dreaded.

"I am going down to Duffin's this evening to take the basket back," he said to his wife.

"I can take it," she said, "I'm going to Skegland's."

"No," he said, "I should like the walk."

She said no more, having only spoken to assure herself of his purpose. She was glad he was going; for, little though she had said of it, and though even in her own mind the thought lacked definite words, she knew that about that time that she heard on Wold Hill at sunset was something utterly wrong.

Rather than postpone what he feared the vicar started sooner than necessary, and came to the farm while the sun was still some way from Wold Hill. And there, when Duffin showed him into the parlour, was Mrs. Duffin all ready to receive him, and she had brought in Tommy. They must have seen him coming while some way off.

"I just brought back your basket," said the vicar. He made no effort to stay. He knew that all that could be left to Mrs. Duffin. And sure enough, she asked after the eggs. "They were excellent," he said, without waiting to reflect whether he had eaten all six, or any. And from that she went to the hens, and from that she went to her work looking after them, and from that to life in general; while Duffin stood and smiled, and Tommy looked mutinous because of his stiff white collar and because he was sitting indoors. And the vicar sat and listened, sometimes adding a brief remark to the conversation, as a traveller skilful with fires puts a piece of fuel exactly where it is needed. And so the talk went on and the sun neared Wold Hill.

And Tommy began to shuffle and grow impatient. After a while the vicar, watching Mrs. Duffin, saw her notice the shufflings. At that moment he rose to go. Mrs. Duffin, who valued gossip with the vicar even a little more than gossip for its own sake, would have tried to delay him in any case, and she did so now if only to reprove Tommy. Thus pressed with a double eagerness the vicar stayed on; and the sun went lower and lower.

The talk was now of onions: how to grow them, how to cook them, and whether they might be eaten raw. For some while Tommy's shufflings had ceased; his expression was changing. A drawn look made his face thinner, his cheeks were paler; but in his eyes, when the vicar looked, was the real change: such a glare of yearning was in them, that the antimacassar[1] behind the boy's head and the black sofa on which it rested seemed suddenly absurd to the vicar. "Yes," thought the vicar, "that boy could do it." For he seemed all changed.

"I think the healthful properties of spring onions," he said, "should outweigh the censure[2] of our neighbours."

"I do so agree with you, sir," said Mrs. Duffin, "but I've always been a little afraid, people being what they are."

"Too censorious, of course," said the vicar quite absently. And there was Tommy Duffin with that look on his face and the sun touching Wold Hill, and shadows huge and long stalking into the valley, and Tommy's left hand moving again and again toward his jacket pocket and drawing back furtively.[3]

---

[1] An ornamental or decorative covering for the back or arms of a chair or sofa to protect it from grease, dirt, and hair oils.

[2] Severe disapproval.

[3] Secretively, as if not to be noticed.

ch. ends next p.

"Oh, yes," Mrs. Duffin was saying, "I think the Cochin Chinas[4] are the best, considering the work they do."

"Yes," said the vicar. And then, feeling sure that the boy would soon be gone and that there would be no overtaking him, he shot out a question that might hit or miss, but was better than doing nothing. "What kind of flute is that," he said, "that you have in your pocket?"

The boy went white.

"I've no flute," he said.

"Come, Tommy," said Mrs. Duffin, "show Mr. Anwrel, whatever it is."

There was a silence, and a stillness came over Tommy. He wore a menacing look, and Anwrel thought he would defend his pocket to the last. Then all in the silence, the light now a little dim, Tommy Duffin, menacing still, drew something out of his pocket.

"What have you got, dear," said his mother, the dark oak of the room making things darker there than they should be just after sundown.

"Why, it's one of those things," said Duffin, "that the Punch and Judy men play.[5] Did you get it . . . "

But the look on the face of Anwrel checked him. For a wild fancy unbidden was crossing the vicar's mind, saying against all reason, "The very pipes of Pan."

---

[4] An historical exonym (an established, non-native name), primarily referring to the population of the southern region of modern-day Vietnam, particularly during the French colonial period.

[5] Punch and Judy is a traditional British slapstick puppet show performed by a single puppeteer featuring Mr. Punch and his wife Judy.

The Air of Brighton[1]

Tommy Duffin had slipped away from the horsehair sofa and parlour, and the vicar had made his farewells, and here he was in the gloaming hurrying home. He had seen at a glance that the pipes young Duffin had shewn[2] him had been probably made by the lad himself, as his wife had actually said, from reeds that he could have got in the small stream running through Wolding. The vicar had no crazy or pagan thoughts concerning them. And yet that one wild fancy that had gone as a flash through his mind, to be instantly banished, by reason, had left like a kind of track, a boding faint but oppressive, that pervaded all his moods and lay deep under every thought; so that he hurried uphill, struggling to be home and amongst familiar things before the tune he dreaded should haunt all the air of the valley. And this he barely did, and was in his study reading a monograph upon eoliths,[3] the worked flints of the brown clay, the crudest tools or weapons of the very earliest men, which he

---

[1] A seaside resort on the southern coast of England.

[2] Archaic spelling of shown (showed).

[3] Roughly chipped flint, once believed to be early stone tool artifacts, but are now recognized as naturally fractured stones.

himself sometimes found in his walks over upland fields, and brought home and kept in a drawer; when there went through the evening that call, a little softened by the walls of the house but multiplied by his ready apprehensions, which drove his thoughts surging far from science and theory, to drift them mazed upon bewildering shores, where nothing in his calling or education could be any guide at all.

In a while the tune died away. How long it lasted the vicar could not guess amongst those tempestuous fancies. But after some seconds or minutes the music died away, and the vicar's thoughts came back guided slowly home by voices from distant gardens, and the chirrup of birds that he knew, and such murmurs as had gone up about that village not only for all the years that he had known it, but for more centuries than one could say. They guided home his thoughts from immense remotenesses as old lights bring shipping home from distant dangerous shores. He wondered how the tune affected others; whether the strangeness that seemed to have come over the parish before he came there absorbed it and made it seem natural; whether minds a little coarser than his were less easily swept afar by it, or whether the plainer minds being closer to natural, even to pagan, things responded to the marvel of that enchantment with an abandonment unknown even to him. He remembered those village maidens gazing at evening toward it.

But his speculations led him nowhere.

It was all silent now on Wold Hill, and gradually Anwrel returned to his only source of comfort, to the thought that all this matter was now in the hands of the Bishop, that a shrewder mind, a far better educated mind, one experienced in the affairs of a hundred parishes, knowing London and (oddly enough so ran the perplexed thoughts) the Athenaeum Club,[4] would see with a wider view this thing that was troubling the parish, and

---

[4] A private members' club founded in London in 1824; primarily a club for men and women with intellectual interests, and particularly (but not exclusively) for those who have attained some distinction in science, engineering, literature, or the arts.

would be able to deal with it wisely. With reiterated hopes that the letter would come tomorrow, Anwrel went to his supper, and soon after that to bed.

And sure enough in the bright morning the letter came. It lay there beside his plate where Marion had put it, an envelope with the Bishop's handwriting. His wife glanced toward him. "Yes," he said, "it has come."

"I'm so glad," she said.

She, also, felt that potent help was at hand.

Then Anwrel read in silence.

And this was the Bishop's letter:

THE PALACE, SNICHESTER,
June 12th.

MY DEAR MR. ANWREL,

You were right to write to me, as at all times, I trust, any clergyman in my diocese[5] will do — and fully — whenever in doubt or difficulty. I can understand your feelings and amply sympathise with them. That your parish is sometimes a little difficult and responds, at times, slowly to the touch on the rein, I knew well; and your letter only confirms the opinion I held, even if your actual statement goes somewhat beyond it. I have, indeed, long been conscious that nearly all the clergy in my diocese are much overworked. Not, indeed, in any one week, not perhaps in a whole year, which makes it so hard to complain; but in a long period of time, year after year with very rarely a holiday, harder worked than the members perhaps of any other profession, and in this diocese especially. And many of my clergy have easier parishes than yours, though some, of course, harder.

Taking into consideration the difficulties of Wolding, and the long time that you have worked there without a holiday, I am especially anxious that you should take a

---

[5] The district or churches under the jurisdiction of a bishop.

holiday (so long delayed) of at least a full week. I am told by one who is especially qualified to judge, that the air of Brighton is particularly invigorating, and he warmly recommends it for the very purpose of rapidly removing all traces of overwork. I will myself see that every arrangement is made for both services in Wolding for at least one Sunday, and I urge you not to return before you feel yourself amply able to cope with all the exigencies[6] of this parish. If I may advise it I would suggest that you should go on your little holiday (of course with Mrs. Anwrel) without any thought for the care that will be taken of Wolding during your absence, for that will be in my hands. My Chaplain will write to you about lodgings he knows of near Brighton, that he believes will be exactly suited to the holiday that we contemplate.

Yours sincerely,
A. M. Wealdenstone.

When Anwrel had read the letter he read it again. Only after that he looked up from it.

"What does he say, dear?" said Mrs. Anwrel.

"He says . . . ," but a weakness came into the vicar's voice, and without saying any more he sat looking foolishly at the letter, and Mrs. Anwrel came round to him and read it. And not a scrap of her disappointment showed in her voice or face as she exclaimed, "Why! He is offering us a holiday."

The tone in which she said it astonished the vicar; for it showed that it was possible for someone to look at this matter as not only not being hopeless, but even as being pleasant; and the possibility cheered him.

"Yes, a week's holiday," he said.

"And this," she said, picking up a letter that had lain under

---

[6] Urgent needs and demands.

the Bishop's, for Marion's eye had swiftly recognised the importance of that one, "this must be the chaplain's."

And so it was.

The chaplain wrote:

DEAR MR. ANWREL,

The Bishop has told me of the holiday that you contemplate taking at Brighton. As I know some rather jolly little lodgings at Hove he thought you would like to hear of them. Hove as you know adjoins Brighton, the esplanade[7] is continuous. The lodgings are kept by a Mrs. Smerdon and she only charges *7s. 6d.*[8] a day for a double-bedded room and board and lodging for two. She has undertaken to do this for any friends of mine, though of course when the ordinary holiday-season is on it brings its temptations for her. I have, however, sent her a note to tell her she must not think of that now, and to make you and Mrs. Anwrel as comfortable as possible. I enclose a list of the trains with their rather tiresome changes, which are, of course, the essence of cross-country journeys. The 3:20 looks the best, does it not? The Bishop tells me that he will be most interested to hear from you as soon as you have completed your holiday. So I assume that you will be writing to him in about a fortnight.[9]

Yours sincerely,
J. W. PORTON.

Standing beside him she had read the letter partly, over his

---

[7] A long, open, level area along which people may walk for pleasure, especially along a shore.

[8] 7 shillings and sixpence. (In British "old money" there were 20 shillings in a pound and 12 pence in a shilling.)

[9] Two weeks.

shoulder, till they arrived at the bottom of the page at different moments and he had read the rest aloud to her.

"Seven-and-six?" she said. "Seven-and-six for everything?" Then suddenly she stopped and said no more about that.

"Yes. It seems very little," he said.

"Yes, it does rather," she answered.

He might have had many holidays. But he did not look on the work that he did amongst those hills as thousands must look on theirs; selling something perhaps that they know to be bad, amongst surroundings against which all the emotions they have are constantly in rebellion; a thing to be fled from as Lot fled from Gomorrah,[10] when rare opportunity offers; alas, to return again. More and more every year the outlines of those hills rounded off for him the view, dreams, outlook, and philosophy that a man calls his world, and so gently rounded it that there could have been nothing in all their slopes to jar on a simple mind.

And more and more every year it grew distasteful to him even to contemplate the fuss and the petty difficulties of leaving that wide circle of hills, wherein everyone knew everyone, for the hurried ways of people who not only would not know him but who with hasty ignorance would assign to him some personality ludicrously unlike his own, and would quietly ridicule or suspect him for every departure they were capable of observing from this absurd personality. And the less he travelled the less did nature equip him with a cynicism that would have been an armour against all this.

His daily, weekday work may be said to have been concerned with all the times of intensity that his neighbours knew; not only when they mourned or when they wed, but when the cricket-team won a notable local match or when they were badly beaten. After such occasions there would often be a smoking-concert, and the vicar would be there. On some such evening of victory none spoke like the vicar. To begin with

---

[10] Genesis 19

he would mention every member of the team and something heroic they had done, or some resolution they had shown in the face of impossible odds, a perfectly new ball for instance from the hand of "their" best bowler, with such work on it as could only be got when the seam was fresh and rough, in fact the first ball of the match; on these lines he brought comfort when there was not material for praise. And praise he handled until each man glowed. It was far better than beer. And from the praise of individuals he came to the occasion itself. And this he spoke of, if there had been a victory, without actual exaggerations, far less with misstatements, and yet in such a way that those who heard him felt that there had been achieved in that valley at last an event that the years had had in gradual preparation, and there grew in the mind's eye of all a glory about Wolding. And if there had been a defeat, then he fixed those mental eyes on some future day, toward which by arduous training and by keeping the eye on the ball that team would assuredly climb to merited victory; and the glory about Wolding would be as vivid as ever. And when you consider, though it is better not, but *if* you consider, how near the paths of life come at times to the edge of that desert that Solomon saw, where all is only vanity,[11] then how wise seem the simple fancies of this man who so often built up for other simple men a triumphant purpose for Wolding. A holiday from all this at any time had a touch of exile about it, but now that this perplexity had arisen, a queerness stranger than any of those he had known in his time in Wolding, he was more loath than ever to turn his back upon it. Yet here was the letter from his Bishop, and one from the Bishop's chaplain, telling him that he had already decided to go. He regretted part of the letter that he had written; he felt that he had exaggerated the difficulties of Wolding, all but this one great difficulty that he longed to stay and cope with. There may have been things now and then that were a little strange, but nothing he could not cope with without the help

---

[11] An allusion to Ecclesiastes 1 (traditionally attributed to King Solomon).

ch. ends next p.

of the Bishop, until this thing came. And how was he to cope with this by going away from it?

His wife saw some of his perplexities. She knew he would not dream of disobeying the Bishop. So the sooner the start was made the better. She woke him out of his reverie with a question about trains.

"Shall we go by the 3:20 today?"

It was that that awoke him with a shock. But it made him realise that he was really to leave Wolding for a while; and after that it was easy for him to decide, and they settled on the 3:20 the following day.

It only remained to write to the Bishop and pack. "I will tell him what I found out about Tommy Duffin," he said.

"No," she said, "he will not want to hear that yet. He expects a long letter from you when we get back."

All in the bewilderment of the approaching move and the packing, he bowed his head to this though he did not understand it. Those that have travelled in Africa, beyond roads and paths and tracks, and know that whatever trifle they leave behind they will have to live without for weeks or months, will the most easily appreciate Elderick Anwrel's anxieties when the matter of packing began. Brighton seemed further to him than Africa does to some of us, and the journey more intricate; yet there is a certain parallel.

Briefly he wrote to the Bishop and brieflier still to his chaplain; and soon he was wholly engrossed by the anxieties and fatigues that are inseparable from the manual labour of packing, aggravated by the strain of sending the imagination on ahead to contemplate all the possible needs of a holiday; and holding it there at its trivial task, as weary as the labour of knees and hands.

5

A Hint from the Wind

The Anwrels had caught the 3:20 at Mereham Station,[1] had changed at Seldham and again further on, and had arrived at Brighton and driven to Hove[2] and found Mrs. Smerdon's lodgings. And there they had late tea in a small comfortable room amongst bound volumes of forgotten magazines; while in Wolding a westering sun was streaking the slopes of Wold Hill with the shadows of thorn and bramble, wild rose and Tommy Duffin. He sat there motionless amongst that wild company, the green dwellers on Wold Hill, gazing across the valley so fixedly and so long that one might have thought there was something strange to see. But there was nothing to see but the glint of the grasses changing the look of the slopes, and distant windows one by one beginning to flame in the rays, and a shadow going up from amongst dark elms, gradually over the downs,[3] till only the woods at the top saw any sunlight; and

---

[1] Another Dusany invention, whose name was surely inspired by Dereham Station, in the English county of Norfolk.

[2] A seaside resort in East Sussex, England; it is one of the two main parts of the city of Brighton and Hove.

[3] Downlands; areas in England of open chalk hills, largely turfed with grass.

then that too was gone and there only remained a glow in the upper air, and a light on the breasts of pigeons passing home.

It was nearly a year since Tommy Duffin had first gone alone to that hill. On one of the last days of August, the first of the days on which, like a prophecy, some hint of the coming of Autumn had gone through the air, he had first felt the lure of the hill all of a sudden at evening. In the foreground of all his thoughts was a weariness at the whole routine of his life, aggravated because it was Sunday; and then there rose up as it were behind this mood the thought of the great dim hill, and the feeling that there all his puzzles might be explained, by the sudden discovery of some purpose that none seemed to know in the village. So he slipped from the house in the valley, and before his father or mother knew he had gone he was away to the hill. As he went through the village it was light enough for him to recognise faces, but darkness began to grow as he climbed the slope. Amongst the wild bushes by which he was sitting now he had sat down and gazed across the valley. And there was the mystery that he had come to find gazing back at him from the opposite side, but silent, hushed, as it were with finger on lip, and not quite to be seen because it was over the top of the hill and just the other side of the shaws[4] of oak. He had gazed long at these trees dark on the crest of the hill on the eastern side of the valley, but could not see the mystery lurking there; which if seen could have told him, as he felt in his heart, not only the purpose of the generations of men that lived their span in Wolding, but the reason even of the ring of old stones that lay in a little valley beyond the ridge behind him, growing moss year after year and casting useless shadows round and round on the plough.[5] They were called The Old Stones of Wolding.

And then he had brought his gaze down the hill, away from the shaws of oak, after wistful and vain searching; and there

---

[4] Small groups of trees.
[5] British spelling of plow.

was the mystery that the darkening trees had hid, lurking now amongst the houses of the village, and almost peering over the ledges of windows where yellow panes were frowning under low eaves. Nor had he found it there, nor on the slope where small wild feet below him were beginning to patter abroad through the whispering grass. And then he had turned to the ridge of Wold Hill above him, where the sky was glowing like a turquoise lantern faintly lit by one candle, where the edge of the wood showed near and ebon[6] black. There, so near that it seemed menacing, the mystery beckoned him from the other side of the hill. He rose and went through the wood; and it was not there. And all the valley, and the great hills fondling it, and the woods and the wild briars, the silence and the sounds that strayed across it, the huge blue circle of the Evening Star,[7] and the whole dome of the night, all seemed intensely to mean something that had no meaning. But when the vast evening, with all its whispers and silences, from the lurking-places of small wild things of the wood to the paths of the wandering stars, still seeming about to utter some ancient secret, still said to him never a word, he had turned at last and gone all dis-consolate home. And amidst all the beauty of that starry night the disconsolate feeling remained with him. He had passed unheeding by the glowworm's light, for those tiny travellers still went lit through the fields; and along lanes, roofed over and scented by the wild clematis,[8] he hurried on uncaring. In the valley a smell of wood-fires came through the damp of the mist, mellow windows glowed; sometimes the thunderous mass of an elm rose over him in its blackness; but he had not seemed to notice. Instead, one thought was echoing in his mind. The purpose? The purpose? What was it all for? The huge evening knew, and it had not told him. Reasons he had been given,

---

[6]　A literary way of saying ebony.

[7]　The planet Venus, seen shining in the western sky after sunset.

[8]　A climbing ornamental plant of the buttercup family which bears showy white, pink, or purple flowers.

ch. ends p. 30

religious and secular. But there was something the evening knew and had not told him.

Next day that feeling persisted, and all the morning he had brooded silently, doing his work in the fields. Now there was an old woman named Mrs. Tichener, who sometimes did the scrubbing at the farm, and her he had known all his life; one of his very earliest memories being of bringing her a bundle of flowers, and weeping when he found out that the weeds had got thrown away, a trouble that had been soothed away for him at last by Mrs. Tichener, as so many others had been. And he always remembered one day when he had asked her some simple question about life, when it was all new to him; (one of his questions had been "Why do dogs bark?" It may have been that one;) and she had given him some quaint reason; and he had asked her how she knew; and Mrs. Tichener had answered "Because I know everything."

Whatever the old woman knew, or whatever was hid from her, she at least had the confidence of the child; for he had not only remembered that remark all these years, but it had always coloured his estimate of her, so that she seemed to him a very wise old woman. To her he had gone that day from the stooks[9] of wheat, and had found her in a small garden sitting beside her hollyhocks,[10] and had put his trouble before her, his longing to roam to the hill, his discontent with his home. And at first she gave him for comfort conventional phrases, and old worn moralities. But he needed something more. For if old women gossiping at evening as the ages go by, spin wisdom as the spider in old barns spins gossamer,[11] then Mrs. Tichener had a great store of wisdom, in which little ancient facts were

---

[9] A group of sheaves (bundles of grain stalks tied together after reaping) stood upright in a field in order to air-dry.

[10] A tall Eurasian plant of the mallow family, widely cultivated for its large showy clusters of white, yellow, red, or purple flowers.

[11] A fine film of cobwebs spun by small spiders often seen caught on bushes or grass, or floating in the air in calm weather.

caught up as is dust in the spider's web. And if these things are all vanity, what are we?

So he questioned her again and again, taking no comfort from anything that she said, when it was such as others might have told him. And then she said, "It was all the fault of that there Reverend Davidson, him that married your father and mother."

And no more of this would she say; but when he pressed her went rambling away from the point down copybooks-full of old sayings. And for having got this much he was cross at not getting more, and all of a sudden strode petulantly away. "Mind my hollyhocks!" she said.

He had gone again to the hill in the dusk, and still got no answer. And then one day when he felt that things were bad at home, and he was still cross with Mrs. Tichener, he went for consolation down to the stream.

And the stream went by in a hurry, perturbed as his own thoughts, yet somehow seeming to care nothing for that. It seemed to have more to show him than downs or wood, for not only had the stream its pebbles and glittering sand, and the light things slipping by on innumerable journeys, but it had also borrowed the sky. He listened long to it, hushed and without moving; when just as it sounded as though it were about to speak to him, it slightly waved one or two bulrushes and went on with its chatter, as a man with the back of his hand might slightly brush documents while speaking of other things. That almost furtive sign, while the babble of water continued as though nothing else had happened, caught the lad's awed attention. Somehow it seemed that the stream had told him more than Mrs. Tichener would: from such slight hints as this is knowledge at times to be gained. He gazed at the bulrushes, but could not find out what it was that the stream had told him.

And those autumn days went by; and the more that he thought of that mystery that always lurked on the wrong side of the hill or hid in patches of dusk, the mystery to which the stream would only beckon and of which Mrs. Tichener would

ch. ends next p.

say no more, the more his father and the young men of the village found him defective in such work as went with other thoughts or with mere industry and punctual habits. The more that the hill called him the more he was scorned by the valley.

He went again to the bulrushes. And then one day, whether on affairs of the autumn or following some quest of its own, a wind sang in the reeds, almost saying to Tommy Duffin what the stream would not say; and ceased, like everything else, before it quite told him anything. And yet its song that was so brief in the reeds remained long in his mind. And there came a day when he went with his knife and cut one of the great rushes, and all the reeds of the stream seemed to be nodding their heads. And guided by some strange lore that seemed older than all the village, he cut it to different lengths and shaped them and bound them together. It was so that he made those pipes that Elderick Anwrel saw.

The Old Stones of Wolding

When Tommy Duffin had those pipes he used to go down to the stream whenever he felt lonely, or puzzled, or at cross purposes with all the ways of the village; and there he used to croon a few low notes, as though the pipes could say something that the wind would not say, something at which the stream only beckoned, and at which Mrs. Tichener stopped suddenly short; but he crooned the notes softly for fear someone should hear and ask him what he was doing. And the soft notes of the pipes brought him some consolation for knowing nothing of that solemn purpose with which the evening vibrated, and with which Wold Hill seemed to thrill, from the ring of old stones behind it to the foot of the slope that watched Wolding. But the notes that consoled him told him nothing at all of the message that the gloaming had for him, of which to his daily sorrow he could read never a word. And so he had fretted and consoled himself and said nothing about his pipes, and breathed so softly upon them that no one heard. And then one day at sunset the hill called him again clearly.

His father sat smoking by the fire and reading a paper, while his mother talked to Tommy. At first he could not get away unnoticed, but sat waiting his opportunity and thinking of only that, like some wild creature shut into a woodman's hut. His mother would soon go out to feed the dog, and he watched the minute hand of the clock until he could see it moving. And still she did not go. And he dared say nothing to remind her. At last she went, and Tommy went out with her. In the open air and dim light he soon slipped away, and so was off to the hill.

Doors in the village were open as he went by, showing cheery interiors all bathed in light; but these were not for him, for whatever had called him was something older than lamp-light. A window glowed, through which he saw two men at a game of chess; but chess was to Tommy Duffin what it was to his father, no more than material for the jokes of his favourite comic paper about the length of time it took. This was nearly the last house, and then the bulk of the hill rose up all dark before him.

Soon he came to the wild-rose bushes high on the slope, like a company of the things of the wild, halted before the village and coming no nearer. Coming no nearer yet; perhaps one day to pour in, following up the retreat of man. He sat down amongst them and gazed over the valley. The mystery was there, but further and fainter than ever. Yet a certain look that there was in the sky behind him, though the look was almost concealed by the tops of the trees, made him feel that what he sought might be just over the hill. So he rose at once and went upward, and came to the dark of the wood; and a track that he dimly saw guided him on, except when everything was blotted out by the immense blackness of yew trees.[1] So dark it grew that sometimes he struck matches, but against this the night seemed to protest as though her dim ways were profaned by it, and the darkness trebled[2] against him the moment the matches faded; and soon he struck them no more. He came over the top of the hill and saw the track more clearly than

---

[1] Evergreen trees which produce red berrylike fruits, and are linked with folklore and superstition.

[2] Tripled; multiplied threefold.

when the slope was before him in all its blackness: stars peered down now between branches: and then he went down the far slope through the dark of the pines. And just when it seemed at its blackest their trunks began to detach themselves from the darkness, blackening it one by one; and then he came to the other edge of the wood, and saw in the West the last faint fragment of day, with the enormous shapes of dark clouds riding insolently across it, and heard dogs far away barking in other valleys. Below him in the dark lay the Old Stones of Wolding.

He went down until he could see them, twelve upright forms shaped of blackness, and amongst them a thirteenth, prone; huge and flat in their circle. He stood amongst them all in the hush, under stars and one huge planet. And it was there that the mystery seemed about to speak, and answer the questions that would not let him rest; when a glow appeared on the ground far off: a farmer was going round his byres[3] with a lantern, and the light disturbed his geese. The geese complained and warned for three or four minutes; and the silence on the Old Stones after that seemed to have settled down for the night.

They would tell him nothing now. When Tommy Duffin was sure of this he turned back up the hill. He came to the wood again and went slowly on through the darkness, the feet of little creatures smaller than rabbits pattering away from his path. On the downward slope looking toward Wolding the huge gnarled roots of trees sometimes made steps for him. And suddenly he came to the starlight again, and the grassy slope and wild-rose bushes. And looking across the valley, full of silence and darkness, beyond the winking windows to the far slopes mute as the rest, all roofed over with stars that followed their silent courses as meaningless to him as Space, he felt he never should learn the mystery now. And a melancholy rose up in him and he took his pipes, and put them for solace to his lips, and blew on them clear and loud, as he had not blown before, a tune that all of a sudden ran in his mind.

---

[3] Sheds or barns for cows.

ch. ends p. 36

And the tune was the answer to all things. What those clear notes said to him he could never put into words; perhaps no man could. But while the music thrilled from his pipes, and while the echoes haunted the air, all his longings were gathered in peace before one enormous answer, and nothing seemed strange or perplexed him any more, and all the mysteries over the ridges of hills seemed near and familiar and friendly, and he knew himself one of a fellowship to which the hush of the night, the deep of the woods, or mysteries bold in the moonlight or hidden by mist, reported all their secrets.

When the tune was over old questionings came back to him, and the mystery withdrew itself further away from his guesses, and all was as unfathomable as ever. Yet not a question he could ask of the night, not a secret the darkness hid, not a quest of the little wild feet in the whispering grasses, but had been answered, revealed and made known to him a few moments before. And the knowledge that this had been, and might be again, calmed him with a great calm.

What had the answer been? He sat there wondering, knowing only that it had come to him. The still night said nothing. A silver streak overhead, a meteorite fell. Glowworms[4] shone at their posts. A grasshopper began to call. Then he put the pipes to his lips again, and the tune answered everything; but so far did it transcend any words of man that nothing remained in his reason, when the echoes had floated away, to tell him how it was that for a little while all secrets were open to him, from the purpose of the Old Stones of Wolding to the emotion that sustained the grasshopper's call.

Dogs barked in the village, and continued to bark long afterward. Men looked up from their papers, or games of cards, and wondered, and thought that they had heard wrong. Girls heard it, and trusted their ears, and knew that they had heard it. Heard what? They did not trouble to stay to answer that. They turned to their mothers. And one said "May I go across and see

---

[4] Fireflies or lightning bugs.

Mary Meriton?" And another "I promised to go and see old Mrs. Skegland." And another "May I go and see if the calf is all right?"

As many of them as could steal away to the hill went searching to find the piper among wild-rose bushes and bramble. And that night none of them found him. For he slipped away from the hill, fearing he might be discovered, while the wonder of the pipes was all new to him, and he feared that they might be wrong. He did not go down to the village, but went away northward along, the face of the hill, so that none should find him if they came up from below. And so he came to a lane low under great hedges, and darkened by the towering growth of wild clematis. The white pathway scarcely glimmered in all that blackness. Here he paused and took off his boots, for the noise of them in the still night irked him. Somehow in his bare feet he felt a little closer to that mystery of which the pipes were the clue.

The lane was unfamiliar to him, for it was far out of his way. He went without a sound, walking on smooth chalk, along the base of the huge black hedge on his left, feeling all alone and one with the hush and wildness of night. Suddenly, right through the clematis, just over his head, a window glowed from an upper room of a house that seemed to be only a few yards in from the lane. That sudden glow, so near, surprised the lad, and he stood quite still and watched it. It made him feel somehow lonelier. Once more something out of the night seemed to be puzzling him. So he sat down under the bank and put the pipes to his lips, and played the strange notes of that time again very softly. And somehow the mystery of that window alone in the night seemed answered. Then he went on down the lane and out into starlight, and came to a road and followed it, still going northward, till he met one going down into the valley to a little bridge over the stream, his boots still in his hand and the pipes in his pocket. Soothed, and at ease at last, he was nearing the village now from the opposite end from that by which he had left it. But behind the window that glowed through a space

ch. ends next p.

in the clematis a girl who was parlourmaid[5] in the little villa was peering into the night with a new and strange agitation. The little lawn was in a glow of lamplight flowing out from the drawing-room below her, because no one had drawn its curtains against the evening. So it could not be from the lawn that those soft notes rose to thrill her. Mrs. Airland, the old lady reading in the drawing-room, heard them too, or she is almost as sure she did as one can be of anything. She got up and went to the window and looked out over the lawn, to the left and then to the right. And seeing nothing there she went to the bell and rang it, to ask Lily if she had heard anything. For what she had heard, if she really had heard it, was very strange indeed, and, what was worse, sounded quite close. But before the bell rang Lily was out of the house, and down the drive and through the gate that was near to the end of the lane. And when Tommy came out on the road in his bare feet she followed softly as he, and stole after him down to the stream, and could not tell why she followed, but there was something about those pipes so that it could not be otherwise.

---

[5] A maid employed in a private home whose duties are to care for the parlor (a room for receiving visitors and entertaining guests) and to answer the door.

7

The Call of Wold Hill

Next day there was talk of the pipes. Everyone in the village had heard them. Those clear emphatic notes had pierced into parlours, amongst talk, amongst games of cards, making the talk all of a sudden seem trivial, or the game pointless, till the room felt stuffy and its ornaments mean, and the hill was calling. Men had done no more than pause awhile in a sentence, or hang longer than usual over playing a card, or a tale was checked in a public-house[1] while men wondered for half a minute, then all had gone on as before amongst the men. But next day there was talk amongst them about what the strange notes could have been.

Of the girls only five or six had been able to slip away from the village, and these had found nothing, and had come back late, with burrs and dew on their dresses, and had sat silent till bedtime. But the others heard too, and remained for long after thinking, and telling their thoughts to none. They too were talking next morning about the music: the whole village was talking: but the girls and the men did not talk about it together.

[1] A tavern or pub.

When any man spoke of it to a girl she pretended not to have heard the tune or not to be interested, though her mind was glowing with it. And, for all the talk in the village, only one person guessed who made that music and only one person knew. Mrs. Tichener, who eighteen years ago had chanced to see something in the vicarage garden that perhaps no other eye had seen for over a thousand years, guessed it was Tommy Duffin, and Lily from the little villa at the end of the hill knew. Lily knew, and became the first disciple of the strange new heresy;[2] heresy as it certainly was to the vicar, strange, as it was to all, and new, as it seemed in spite of the ages of its antiquity, to all but those who turned back very far the pages of that blend of fable and history that tells the story of Man.

And the talk going through the village soon came to Duffin's farm, and was a topic awhile for his conversation with Mrs. Duffin at dinner, for both thought they had heard it; while Tommy sat and listened, his opinion not being asked. After that Tommy went to his room to a deep old box, and hid the pipes far down under all his possessions, a varied heap too untidy for anyone to disturb; and there the pipes lay safe all through the autumn. And as the year wore on a haze began to appear in the valley at evening, the thinnest veil through which the grassy slopes shone a pale gold. Tommy, driving the cart full of sheaves[3] to the barn, felt the lure of those pale gold slopes and the glamour of evening, yet he would not go again with his pipes to the hill; for all the talk there had been about that music that suddenly came to him had made him anxious, and he was afraid of being found out doing what as yet was as strange to himself as it was to the folk who had heard those curious notes ring through their parlours.

The thistledown[4] blew by, trusting in light winds, the little speck of life within it probably lit by some tiny hope of soft earth somewhere and splendid growth; a hope, if the little speck of

---

[2] A controversial belief or opinion contrary to orthodox religious doctrine.

[3] Bundles of grain stalks tied together after reaping.

[4] The light, fluffy, and feathery down attached to the seedlike fruit of a thistle.

inferior life was able to hope at all, less vain than many of ours. There came up the valley one day from the South the last thunderstorm of the year, with rain at its vortex, where thunder was closest to lightning, that washed gravel down sloping paths and buried it under the sand of hundreds of little estuaries.[5] The stream rose as in dreams at evening and filled the whole valley, four hundred feet deep and nearly two miles across, with the phantasm of a mighty river: it was only its dream, only the white mist. Brown fields were bare of their sheaves. The foliage of potatoes was rotting. Blackberries were ripe. And all was ready for the year's second wonder, the leaves' last glory before their farewell to the woods, and their long deep sleep in the forgetting earth. And Tommy Duffin dared not go to the hill, and there came back slowly his old dissatisfied mood, the questioning and the wonder that only his pipes could answer. Only his pipes: the first few trees that turned, like scouts stolen into the valley in front of some golden army, gave him merely hints, not answers. And all the pomp[6] of the departing year told him of some transcendent thing in a language he could not read. Gold and red in the woods, whatever autumn was writing; the mystery of owls' voices, whatever old tale they were telling; the long grey script of the mist, written on air; were in no language he knew. Only his pipes spoke it.

And winter came, and spoke in a brilliance of stars, and with blazing sunsets prophesied, boding strange things; and geese, foreknowing the storms, forsook distant seas, and came over high, a wandering letter V. And one wild evening Tommy's disconsolate wonder overcame his shy fear, an evening without a splendour about the sunset, the huge sun dropping enormous below the dark of the hill, unattended by any glory besides his own monstrous magnificence. In the hush of that evening Tommy went to the hill.

He sat on the crisp cold grass and looked at the night. The

---

[5] An estuary is the end of a river where its mouth meets the sea.
[6] Splendor.

ch. ends p. 42

trees were intensely black and intensely still, each one of their upper twigs stretched rigid against the sky, sombrely prophesying he knew not what. And once more he put his pipes to his lips and blew. And a tune welled up inspired by a magic he knew not, that was older than all those trees, a primaeval thing crooning a tale to the sleeping valley; and it seemed so old in a knowledge of dreams that had troubled men that it almost sounded human; and yet the notes that came out of those pipes of reed were more like those of strange birds with enchanted voices than any notes of men, and called to mind no tune that any knew. They heard it in the village. Suddenly the ornaments in their parlours went tawdry;[7] their walls seemed suddenly narrow, the lamplight garish, their work a weary thing, and again the hill was calling. For some seconds they all stood silent, the lure drawing their hearts; then many of them put the lure away, and turned back to other things, with a new dissatisfaction, scarce felt perhaps, yet lying heavy in the deeps of the heart. But many did not put the lure away, but went to the hill and crept near to Tommy Duffin, and lurked among thorn and bramble to see if he played again; and Lily came up the lane where the clematis hung, and found him and sat beside him. And he played again and the strange tune thrilled through those listeners, eight girls that had escaped from the tidy village, and Lily from the house at the end of the hill, from the old lady who sat once more wondering as she had not wondered for years. Then doors began to open down in the village; light streamed from them, and there was the sound of a stir; and Tommy Duffin was gone. He went up the hill as wild things go at night, disturbed by wayfaring men. He came to the wood, and putting once more the pipes of reed to his lips as he lightly moved through the blackness, he blew one challenge or taunt on behalf of the thing that inspired him, against all that was orderly in the affairs of men, though knowing nothing of what that inspiration was. That too was heard in the village;

---

[7] Gaudy or cheap in appearance.

and women there, too old to go to the hill, opened windows and gazed at the wood, then swiftly threw out antimacassars or tea-cosies,[8] all in a sudden petulance at their smugness. But Tommy ran on through the wood, and going far round stole home by another way.

Next morning the talk of the pipes, which had only died down a few weeks before, rose in greater volume than ever, sweeping all other topics away, drowning the light gossip of yesterday like dead leaves. And it was more than mere talk; there were conjectures in it; each one that he heard seeming nearer to Tommy Duffin, until one to his great relief, seemed further away. Even the vicar had heard it, right over the valley; Tommy wondered that the notes could have travelled so far. Everywhere the question "What was it?" And Tommy going about in moody silence; till he feared that his silence was in itself suspicious, and he began to ask questions too and make foolish guesses. Nor need he have disguised his guesses much; for what did he know of this strange spell that had hold of him, or whence it came, or what the music was that could answer the riddles of evening and solve the mystery that haunted the hills at night, and leave the human heart soothed and at ease for that solving? Yet he feared they suspected him. What should he say when they asked him why he did it. He that did not even know.

But he need not have feared. They looked for somebody leaner and darker than him, somebody stranger and older; slightly foreign. The picture of the player of those pipes was strangely alike in the minds of all that heard them, olive-brown skin, dark hair and nimble limbs, eyes dark and keen and an almost goat-like profile, strangely unlike Tommy Duffin. He need not have feared, yet he put his pipes away, and played then on the hill no more that winter. But when Spring appeared; at first with a gathering of anemones,[9] like a multitude of the

---

[8] Knit or cloth coverings for a teapot used to keep its water warm.

[9] A perennial plant of the buttercup family, typically bearing large brightly colored flowers.

ch. ends next p.

fairy folk, that had marched to the wood from elfland, pale people all just flushed with the wonder of Spring; then with the blue flood of the hyacinths, like pieces of sky lured downward by a witch of the deeps of the wood; and lastly with all the scent and splendour of may; when Spring appeared and all the birds were fluting, and the blackbird chorus woke Tommy Duffin each morning before it was light, and his heart and the hills were alike enchanted with wonder, then he cared no more nor thought what any would say, but took his pipes at sunset and went up to the hill, and played once more the tune that answered the evening. And again he went next day, and many days after, and the maidens of the village gathered at evening in a kind of crescent on the slope just below him; and the village filled with rumours as strange as the tune, so that some of them even came to the ears of the vicar. And travellers from London that chanced that way; probably by a wrong turning from the great Arnley road,[10] for Wolding's road led nowhere; as the quiet wheels of their bicycles slipped downhill through the village, heard snatches of conversation that would have strangely puzzled them, and would have made a strange tale for the world's idle ear, and this tale of mine would have been old; but they put it all down to the natural inferiority of country people, and so forgot about it. And Spring went by with all these rumours growing, and the pipes, as it seemed, more insolent every evening, more defiant of all those illusions to which we rightly cling, till the vicar knew it was time to write to the Bishop.

And now Tommy sat on the hill with his pipes in his hand a little while before sunset, afraid no longer of anyone in the village or of what they might ask or say, meditating fiercely and curiously, while the Anwrels sat at a table in Mrs. Smerdon's parlour in front of a tea-cosy that she had embroidered herself.

---

[10] Another Dusany invention, likely inspired by Armley Road in Leeds, England.

The Reverend Arthur Davidson

The novelty of Brighton might long have entertained anyone that came to it as new as the Anwrels did. There were three great things to see that were unfamiliar to Anwrel. There was first of all the sea; and all that expanse untouched by the care of man had an almost soothing effect on a simple mind long accustomed to contemplate in any view a series of humble triumphs, only won from Nature by constant labour and care. And then there was the town, the royal monument to a bygone holiday, with its great modern hotels amongst which the Anwrels were as out of place as a Swiss hall-porter would have been at the hop-picking.[1] And behind all this were the downs, that had once looked straight at the sea, face to face, with nothing between them, and would again; the South downs that the vicar did not know, but they reminded him pathetically of those that he knew to the North, and only a glimpse of them was enough to bring back his thoughts to the trouble from which

---

[1] A Swiss hall-porter refers to a highly formal hotel employee often found in elegant, sophisticated European establishments. Meanwhile, hop-picking was a rustic, seasonal farm activity in the English countryside, typically carried out by working-class families or hired laborers.

they seldom wandered far. For he could not forget the face of Tommy Duffin as he had seen it that evening in the parlour at Valley Farm just as the light was fading. There had been something in it that seemed to menace his parish, either the simple people he loved so well, or the old ways he loved even more. It seemed to menace them; a strong word that, but the right word, thought Anwrel: he had not written strongly enough to the Bishop, and had failed to secure his help; he would write again more strongly, saying clearly all that he feared; he would put it so that the Bishop was bound to help him. For without that help what could he hope to do with a trouble so strange that in his humble career nothing like it had ever come within his experience? Such a thing would have to be dealt with by the Bishop.

It was clear that the Bishop intended Anwrel to stay at Hove for about a fortnight. But how could he do his work there? How could he find out just what it was that was sinister in this thing that was puzzling the village? How find out the harm it threatened and how avert it? No doubt the Bishop had sent some able man to Wolding. A double first at least: the Bishop would know many such. But how much would the newcomer know of what had happened already? If he put everything right before Anwrel came back what a relief that would be. But if he did not! If Anwrel had to do it all by himself, the sooner he got to work upon it the better, lest the thing that he feared should happen. And he did not know what he feared. He must have the facts. He must gather all the information he could about what was going on in Wolding. And for this he must be on the spot. What use in staying at Hove? But he stayed the exact week that the Bishop had ordered.

Some solace he got in that week by reading in Mrs. Smerdon's parlour, for the forgotten magazines were new to him, and some in gazing at the incredible multitude of smooth bright pebbles that the sea had hoarded, useless, as many collections, but shapely and curious and the work of ages. Yet the moment any immediate interest was over, back came again to him that expression on Tommy Duffin's face, and all the calculations that it gave rise to, beginning with wildest phantasy — for what less had he seen in Tommy Duffin's eyes? — then checked and kept within bounds, so far as that was possible, by all such facts as he had come by, and everything leading up to help from the Bishop. And here Mrs. Anwrel found it harder to comfort him, for she doubted if help would ever come from that quarter.

Of Anwrel's weary guesses and calculations I need not tell, for though action is but the shadow cast by thought, yet we follow the shadow more easily than the swift flame that casts it; and the visible result of his anxious wondering was that after seven clear days of exile the Anwrels returned to Wolding, and the vicar brought a pound packet of the best tea he had been able to buy. The return to the vicarage was triumphant: there was the slow and stately welcome of the black cat, a creature brought up with so much kindness that once, on being picked up and carried away from the hearth-rug, it had screamed from surprise; and there was the welcome of the inanimate things, long-familiar knick-knacks that were sparkling now in the sun; and there was Marion hurrying in with the tea, and Mrs. Tweedy the cook coming to ask if they would have cold roast beef for supper, not because there was anything for them to have instead, but because she hoped to hear about Brighton. It was pleasant to be again at their own tea-table; and yet the vicar did not stay for his tea, but hurried down to the village with the packet that he had bought, and ran with it to the house of Mrs. Tichener, where he arrived in time for his purpose, for Mrs. Tichener had not made tea, though the kettle was already singing.

"I've brought you a present from Brighton," he said as he entered.

"Welcome back, sir," she said all at the same time.

"Thank you, Mrs. Tichener," said the vicar. "It's a pound of tea."

"It's very kind of you, sir," she answered.

"I hope you'll like it," he said.

ch. ends p. 49

"That I'm sure I shall," said Mrs. Tichener.

And with a little more talk about the tea the point was easily reached at which she asked the vicar if he would stay and taste it himself.

"But I shall be wasting it. I like it so strong, you know," said the vicar.

And she made it strong, and all had gone according to plan. Then they sat over their tea and talked; and the subject of the talk was the aquarium at Brighton, where the dwellers in many seas gaze through a sheet of plate glass and wonder at men, and men from the other side of it wonder back. And listening to stories of Brighton in the warm room, over the good tea that was stronger than usual, the past began to come back to Mrs. Tichener: she too had stories to tell, and of further away than Brighton, stories of years that were gone. In such a mood as this no tale of wonderful fishes was to be allowed to win; for in conversation as in cards there are winnings and losings, wonder and laughter and even awe are the points. She had her strange stories too; and, gently as the Arab guides his camel with the light cord only on one side of the neck, the vicar guided her reminiscences whither he wished them to go. He had silently progressed some way in his speculations during the last week, and had now come to Mrs. Tichener, believing that the old woman could lead them further. Her gossip was always local; but spreading it over a wider area would have made it no shrewder, nor enriched it much with more knowledge of the whims and the ways of man. They were speaking now of the time of the Reverend Arthur Davidson.

"I often remember hearing, Mrs. Tichener," said the vicar, "how you saw Mr. Davidson one night in the vicarage garden."

"Oh yes, sir," said Mrs. Tichener.

"He was dancing I think," said the vicar.

"Yes, sir. Dancing he was," she said.

"And you told them about it in the village."

"I told a few, sir."

"And then Mr. Davidson left."

"He left at once, sir. Left next day."

"And was never heard of again."

"Not to my knowledge, sir."

"Now that was strange, Mrs. Tichener."

"Yes, it was strange, sir. Strange enough."

"You only told them you saw him dancing?"

"That was all, sir. I don't hold with telling tales about people."

"And yet he left?"

"Oh, yes. He left, sir."

"Well that was all about it I suppose," said the vicar. "There was nothing so very strange in his dancing."

Simple words enough as you see them written, and yet a golden key, a spell to open instantly the lock on the tale of the past that lay in the old woman's mind, a charm to arouse a mystery from its sleep which otherwise might have gone silent in a few more years to the grave.

"Nothing so very strange, sir?" said Mrs. Tichener.

"Oh, not if he cared for dancing," said the vicar.

"Well, sir, you saw queer fishes when you were at Brighton," she said, "but you never saw the like of that."

"Really? Oh? Was it very strange?"

The doubt in his voice drove her onward. He that had brought her strange tales from Brighton should hear strange things now.

"He wore spats,[2] sir," said Mrs. Tichener.

"Yes," said the vicar. "I believe I heard he did."

"And he had a joint, sir, below his spats as he danced."

"Good gracious," said the vicar, awed by her tone. "His ankle of course."

"Yes, sir," she said. "And he had another, just above."

That was her moment of triumph: he had brought no stories like that back from Brighton.

"Good gracious!" he said.

"Yes, sir," said Mrs. Tichener.

---

[2] A cloth or leather gaiter covering the ankle and instep (the top of the shoe where laces normally appear) and fastening under the shoe with a strap.

ch. ends next p.

He had expected the curious events of today to have strange roots back in the past. He had looked for an odd tale from Mrs. Tichener; but not for this!

"And his knees, Mrs. Tichener?" he said.

"I couldn't be sure, sir. They didn't look right as he danced, and he always walked very stiff, but I couldn't be sure. But the joints at each end of his spats, I saw them clear, sir. He was dancing high in the moonlight. Very short boots he always used to wear: neat and small."

"You never saw anything like that before?" asked the vicar.

"No, sir," said Mrs. Tichener. "Quiet and respectable he was always."

"And he went away next day," said the vicar, more to himself than Mrs. Tichener. So she would have no more to tell.

"Well, goodbye, Mrs. Tichener," he said. "And what you've told me, you know, it's best to tell no one else. It would only set them imagining all kinds of things. And it wouldn't do any good."

"I understand, sir," she said, "I keep my tongue to myself. Thank you for the tea. It's very good I'm sure. They must have wonderful things in Brighton."

And with difficulty he withdrew from the tongue that Mrs. Tichener kept to herself.

Tea was all over when he returned to the vicarage; and, as he saw the cold remains and the lonely cup, one of those regrets that will sometimes darken a moment came over him when he saw that he had missed that pleasant meal, the first one of their return after all that week. Yet, even if she saw the shadow that fell on so brief a moment, Mrs. Anwrel saw by some sign that was clear to her that the vicar had won some success on his quest to the village.

"There was something very queer about that man Arthur Davidson," he said.

"They all think so in the parish," she said.

"It was more than that," he said. "Such appearances must

be rare. But how often are they not recognised, or hushed up? It makes them seem rarer."

"What was he?" she said.

"That we shall never know," he answered.

And from this she guessed.

9

The Facts of the Case

The vicar went to his study. And there were the little things with which he had surrounded himself long ago and which he had known for so many years; his quill pens, the knife with which he recut them when they got blunt; his ink-pots with black and red ink, the red for neat headings in his sermons; his collection of eoliths, the old brown debatable stones, whose yellow chippings some argued to be accidental and not the work of man; his palaeoliths[1] with one great blue axe-head that no one could doubt at all; a photograph of himself with ten other young athletes, all on the other shore of a gulf of thirty years; a pottery jar for tobacco that one of them gave him; his comfortable table; and many other small things brought lightly together by him, to become in a while his surroundings, a sort of inner line of defence, of which the Milky Way is the outer, against the drear emptiness of Space. He saw them all as he opened the door: there they were all just as he pictured them

---

[1] Stone tools dating to the Palaeolithic period (c. 3.3 million – c. 11,700 years ago), also known as the Old Stone Age, when primitive man and the manufacture of these tools first emerged.

during every day of his absence; and they seemed too good to be true.

He went in and sat down at the table; and for a while he leaned back in his chair, full of the satisfaction of being again with his own things. Then taking his pen he sat up to the table and wrote, with little more than the savour of that satisfaction still tinging his mood. He wrote again to the Bishop:

"My Lord,

In writing again, in accordance with your lordship's instructions, I am only too conscious of the deficiencies of my former letter. I have since then been able to obtain facts that I ought to have had in the first case, and I have found the week of leisure, that your lordship so kindly gave me, quite admirable for ordering and arranging all the details that I was possessed of which bore on the case. I realise now how necessary this interval was for the adequate preparation of a case that was to be put before your lordship. How strange a case I trust this letter will show.

The most important defect in my former letter was my omission to state, after full enquiry, the precise origin of that music, the nature of which I have already described so far as that is possible to me. It is partly to correct this omission that I now write.

In the first place then there are a farmer and his wife living not far from the village, with one son, living with them, aged about 17. The farmer is of a somewhat simple type, old yeoman[2] stock of this county, with plenty of shrewd knowledge about farming on this particular soil, and without interests beyond that. His wife is really not remarkable in any way. They are both very good church-goers. The son is very like the father, both in appearance

---

[2] A farmer who cultivates his own land, especially in England a member of a former class of small freeholders (persons with an estate in land, inherited or held for life).

and tastes; and I should have said like his mother too, were it not for this one extraordinary thing, for he is the boy who plays the tune on the hill. He has made some strange pipes; and I have seen him with them, and seen him slip away from his father's farm at sunset, and have heard that music soon after. My week at Brighton gave me an admirable opportunity for going over all the facts in my mind, and my careful examination of them there led me to make certain enquiries of an old woman of this parish as soon as I returned this afternoon. Those enquiries have abundantly increased my store of facts that seem to bear on this case. They seem to establish in my mind, though I await your lordship's ultimate decision, that this young man Thomas Duffin, the ordinary son of ordinary parents, has been affected to a terrible degree by some prenatal[3] influence from a perfectly shocking source. What possible curse or spell, or whatever it be, can have been cast over him I will carefully investigate further. But the facts that I have already learned are these. I hardly know how to tell them to your lordship. But the fact is that the Reverend Arthur Davidson, who lawfully married the lad's parents, for there is no doubt that he had contrived to be ordained,"

The vicar held the pen till it nearly dried, then rose and walked about the little room, and still no words would come to him in which to tell what he had to tell to the Bishop. So he went through to the drawing-room and found his wife. "This is what I have written so far, Augusta," he said.

She read the letter slowly.

"Really what I have to tell him," he said, "is so very unusual that I find it hard to choose the right words. But I must do it. He must be told. I wonder if you would be able to word it for me."

"I shouldn't send this letter, dear," she said.

---

[3] Before birth.

"What?" said the vicar. "Not send it?"

"Not quite as it is," she replied.

"But, but it's a thing he must know," he said.

"Then, whatever it is, I should tell him," she said. "Go and see him, you know. But not write."

"But why not write it?" he asked. He relied so much on her sense that he did not question her next remark although it much surprised him.

"I don't think he wants a letter quite like that," she said.

"He doesn't want it?" was all he said.

"I don't think so," she said. "But of course you could tell him verbally."

"But I can't put it clearer than that in conversation: I couldn't put it as clear."

"But you could see how he was taking it," she said.

"Go over to Snichester?" he said.

"I think that's best," she answered.

"Oh dear me," said the vicar. He was thinking of all his friendly, familiar surroundings, and how he must take farewell of his knick-knacks again almost as soon as they had been restored to him.

"You need only go for one night," she said. "You could take the 2:45 and put up at the Crozier."[4]

"If I went in the morning," he said hopefully, "I could get back the same day."

"The afternoon would be the time to see him," she said.

She seemed to know, and he said no more. But, considering the dreadful nature of his news, he did think it a little strange that he should have to give it within conventional hours. He took back his letter and kept it to refer to, for as far as it went it contained his facts. The simple statement of Mrs. Tichener that he had not yet committed to writing he was not likely to forget, and did not in fact forget all the days of his life.

Augusta packed his bag for him. And next day, after a look

---

[4] A clever name for an inn by Dunsany, as a crozier is a ceremonial staff carried by a bishop or an abbot, hooked at one end like a shepherd's crook.

ch. ends next p.

through his eoliths and the fine palaeolithic axe-head, he drove away in his trap[5] to Mereham and the 2:45.

And with him went Spelkins, his gardener-groom, to bring the horses home.

---

[5] A light two-wheeled horse- or pony-drawn carriage.

In the Cathedral

When Anwrel arrived at Snichester it was as yet too early for him to call on the Bishop. Or so his wife had told him. "It must be after four," she had said. So he strolled through the old streets, past several shops of the vendors of genuine antiques, of which there were many important factories in that city.

Soon over one of these shops there appeared a white flash, like a smile, almost contemptuous; and there came into view, as must come to all travellers in Snichester, by whatever street they wander, the great battlements of the cathedral. Anwrel, who was no wayfarer, had never even seen Snichester till that day, and when that row of battlements[1] came into view, as though lifting up sheer out of dreamland, he stood still for a moment and gasped at them. That anything so spiritual could have been made by masons astounded him. For the battlements were made, not of rock, but of pieces of blue sky, lightly framed in white sandstone. To compare all manner of armament, ancient or modern, with Christian virtues he was well

---

[1] The top of a wall, especially of a fort or castle, that has regularly spaced squared openings for shooting through.

accustomed, but to see metaphors made by a mason astonished him; and they were nothing else, for these square pieces of sky, shaped in their thin stone frames like the defences of rugged towers of bygone days, could have averted no material thing. He saw the great green roof, below the towers, making a vivid brightness against the sky, such as we often see all about us just before thunder. He went on until the cathedral stood before him, a great sheet of light glittering from white sandstone, making the very sources of light seem suddenly closer, as though he were standing now at the end of the world. He felt as the hunter or mountaineer may feel as he comes to a mountaintop; though why he felt it he did not know, nor could he even quite have said what the feeling was, except that his emotions had found some altitude from which all the lesser cares seemed tiny and far. Then swifter than feet of hunter or mountaineer those emotions descended, and he was on the pavement gazing; for such altitudes are never for us for long. And the feeling came over him then that would come to him when he had lost something; but he had lost nothing at all, so the feeling was meaningless: there he stood while others went by him by ones and twos to enter the cathedral. Soon he joined their movement through sheer irresolution, as brown leaves seem to go with little runnels;[2] and so came to a small black door that was all one piece of wood, hewn long ago from an oak that bygone men had dragged and carted there over other fields. It was not yet four and he had ample time before he need see the Bishop. He entered, and suddenly was in a coolness and dimness, with splendours of stone and glass that at first bewildered him, till his eye wandering lost along those cliffs of masonry found emblems here and there that had meaning to him. He walked through the gloaming and the hush of the aisles, past old memorials in brass whose antique style seemed speaking sleepily across so many ages, past monuments in stone defaced

---

[2] Small streams, channels, or rivulets in the ground.

so long ago that the very iconoclasm[3] seemed hallowed now, past the quiet sleep of marble, ambition, and dust, his attention almost drowsing in the dim silences, till all of a sudden like thunder he saw a cuirass[4] and helmet once worn at Waterloo.[5] This somewhat woke him, so that he ceased to wander from shadow to shadow of huge pillars, but sat down in one of the pews, and began to order each statement of the report that he had come to make to the Bishop. First of all the facts, to be clearly stated as such; then his deductions, of as much value as the facts, but to be kept separate from them, being a different class of information. He would describe as fully as possible the exact effect of that music upon himself, with no pretence of explaining its full power, but as an example of the impression that it was capable of making upon one mind. And then, having detailed facts, deductions, impressions, he would perhaps go over the ground again, giving briefly the story of the pipes of Wolding as far as he knew it at present. Whether the story he had made of all these facts and impressions were the accurate statement of the case would then be for the Bishop to say: he only hoped that he had exaggerated it.

As he ordered all his facts, carefully distinguishing between them and conjectures, a service began far away from him which he could not see, for the organ interposed between him and the altar where he sat near an end of the nave below a pale ice-blue window. So far off from him was the service in this huge place that it did not at once take his thoughts from their occupation, and he continued to make a clear and logical story of his strange experience in Wolding during the last few weeks. But gradually the distant intonations soaring amongst far pillars lured all his thoughts from the tale he had come to tell. It was not the words that lured him far from his purpose, for he was not able to hear

---

[3] In this context, the destruction of religious images as heretical.

[4] A piece of armor consisting of a breastplate and backplate fastened together.

[5] The Battle of Waterloo was fought on June 18, 1815, near the village of Waterloo (in what is now Belgium), in which Napoleon's army was defeated by the British and Prussians.

ch. ends next p.

them, but a drone as of bees in limes too enormous for this small planet; and, in those colossal trees that the voice awoke in the vicar's imagination, the ages seemed to be caught, humming mildly, with no room in their gentle melody for any tale such as his. He looked round him, trying to gather his thoughts again for the report he must soon make now. He saw a small window showing St. Ethelbruda,[6] beating away the last of the pagans with a branch or a bunch of leaves. He raised his eyes from that to the great windows; one of them seemed like sheer moonlight, another like honey, a third reminded him of dawn, and a fourth baffled him for anything to which to liken it, unless to a great shout. He looked again at St. Ethelbruda in her gay dress beating the pagan; then to the gloom of the pillars; and nowhere could he find any support for the tale that he had to tell. A great bell struck. It was time now to start for the palace; yet the vicar did not rise. It seemed to have all been decided, once for all and long ago, in ritual, in glass and in stone, that this story of his was wrong. If he started at once he could pick up his bag at the station and catch the 5:10, and be home that night, and need not stop at the Crozier. And this was what he did.

---

[6] A fictional saint created by Dunsany.

The Tune in the Twilight

At Mereham the vicar hired a fly,[1] and was home in good time for supper. He explained to his wife that on thinking it all over he found that he had not sufficient information to lay the whole case clearly before the Bishop. And she troubled him with no further questions, seeing that they would have interfered with his great pleasure at being home again. But, supper over, he did not let that pleasure interfere with his duty, for he certainly had to write something to the Bishop. So he went at once to his study and sat down, and jotted down on a sheet of foolscap[2] the simple facts of the case, avoiding very carefully any ominous phrases, and even words that had any sinister import attaching to them. It was a very plain statement that he was putting together. If anything dreadful seemed to hang over it all, or a strange danger to threaten Wolding, it was the Bishop that must put that construction upon it, for the vicar did not even hint at a menace. And now having finished his notes he drew a sheet of writing paper toward him. It was a warm moonlight

---

[1] A one-horse carriage.
[2] A sheet of writing paper measuring approximately 13 by 16 inches.

night, as near as may be to midsummer. It was barely night at all, and a tinge of dawn would appear and awake the blackbirds before the last glow of the sunset was wholly lost from the hill. Scents of flowers from the vicarage garden were wandering down the air.

My Lord [he began]. I have been able to collect certain facts touching the matter upon which I wrote last week.

And then through the air that an owl only rarely disturbed, right through the scents of the flowers, and across the paths of the hawkmoths, went once again the tune that he so much dreaded. As it ripped through the fading twilight it stirred again longings that the vicar had hoped he would feel no more, as though almost, had it not been so absurd, he would have gone away over the hill to dance fantastic dances to a tune that was unlike anything in all music, and unlike any other lure that he knew. The tune ceased all of a sudden, leaving only a few echoes dancing softly along far hills; then silence came where that strange music had been. For a while the vicar's thoughts ran on like the echoes, from cliff to cliff in far places, then he turned back to his letter. How make the Bishop understand?
He took another sheet and wrote thus:

MY LORD,
I am now fully recuperated from any fatigue I may have incurred from my work in this parish. The air of Brighton was most restorative, and both my wife and I have benefited from it greatly. I shall not trouble your lordship further unless anything should ever arise in this little parish of Wolding that should be of sufficient importance to warrant such a step.
I am, my lord,
Your lordship's obedient servant,
ELDERICK ANWREL.

With a sigh he put it into an envelope, addressed it and stamped it, and laid it on the left of his table, where his letters were always put when ready to post. When he turned from it back to his blotting-paper to write to a seedsman about some small need of his garden it was one of those final moments of which History knows nothing, when an episode in a humble life is over.

But Marion broke in before he could take his pen. "Will you want me any more, sir, this evening?" she said. "Because . . ."

He listened to her no further.

"Marion," he said, "have you not a young man in Yorkshire?"

"Yes, sir," said Marion. "But, oh, you could never understand."

Then she was gone.

Marion too. He must fight this out alone. And for that he must know exactly what was against him. His immediate enemy was the awful lure of that music. And the music came from the pipes of Tommy Duffin. Of its ultimate origin he had no longer a doubt. But one thing still remained for him to discover: by what means had the tune been inspired by him that had passed as the Reverend Arthur Davidson?

The Warning

That night when all in Valley Farm were asleep Tommy Duffin crept home through a window, the latch of which he had partly unfastened earlier so that the blade of a knife could open it. It was after midnight and he was fast asleep in his small room over the honeysuckle, when he heard coming clear through dreams the sounds of repeated tapping: Louder the tapping grew and fainter the dreams; until the tapping, which had been no more than one of many realities, all more gorgeous than it, became now the only reality. It was the sound of small gravel upon his windowpane. When it went on and on he opened the window, and there was Lily signing to him to come down.

"Tommy," she said in a low voice when he came, "I heard two young fellows talking when I went home by the lane. I came to warn you about it."

"Talking?" he said heavily for he was barely yet awake and he never had the sharp wits that move swiftly.

"They were talking about you, Tommy. One of them was Willie Latten."

The tone of her voice did more to waken his wits than the words.

"They were planning to stop you going to the hill any more. They don't like you playing to us."

They moved further away from the house, lest anyone should wake up and hear their voices; and came to the meadow where the cattle were lying, dark shapes by the stream, their breath going up pale grey to damp air that lay over the water.

"What are they going to do?" he asked.

But she would not say that they intended to beat him. It seemed too dreadful to her, and she would not say it. For those pipes had taken the place in her heart of all other things, and were sacred.

Instead she said: "Oh Tommy, you must never stop the pipes, never stop playing, never, never. We must go further away where they will not hear you. But they must not stop the pipes."

Yet where was there to go? Others would hear those pipes wherever he went. Tommy was thinking now: his wits were at last awake.

"Are there only two?" he asked.

"No," she said. "All the young fellows are coming. We must go further away."

He did not answer: he was thinking deeply. He had not yet seen the other young men of Wolding while playing his pipes on the hill: none of them seemed as yet to be sure it was he. All the parish had felt the curiously magical lure that there was in the strange music; and the girls had obeyed it without any question and had gone at once to the hill. But the men had thought over it and talked of it, and had not yet gone; and it was lonely for them in the village at evening with all the girls away on the hill in the dark. One or two had crept up the hill to watch, but Tommy Duffin had gone away over the slope and thought that they had not seen him. And now they were all coming. And little wonder. Well, it had to be sooner or later.

"I'm not going further off," he said.

"Tommy, Tommy, you don't understand," she said frantically. "They'll smash the pipes, Tommy."

But he was like a man of genius, if even a little more simple;

ch. ends next p.

like a man with some strange power; and simple though such men be, they would have to be simple indeed if they knew nothing at all of that power, however strange. He knew little enough, and perhaps after all that's all that there is to be known of any of these strange things. Only he knew enough to trust in the power.

"They can't smash the pipes, Lily," he said, and knew not why he had said it. Yet no boast seemed too great for that wonderful music that could answer the riddles of night, and hush the mysteries that lurked upon darkening hills, and seemed to beckon the spirit of man to stray from the paths it knew. She drew a little warmth from his confidence, but she was still all shaken with fear. It seemed to her dreadful that anyone should dare to attack those pipes, or the player upon them, in whom was centred to her all that incomprehensible wonder that rang in the tune; their project to her seemed outrageous and sacrilegious. And if it succeeded! How could she go back then to the drab ways she had known? For all ways of life that she knew, and all that she guessed, seemed equally desolate to her, if Tommy's inspiration should die and the pipes become silent.

"I think they mean to try tomorrow," she said, looking anxiously in his face in the luminous summer night.

There are moments, as when an orator rises to speak, or the big-game hunter looks along the sights of his rifle and two yellow eyes stare back, when all previous fears or anxieties are over and the master's skill has free and exultant play. As hunter or orator might look on the spur of one of those moments, so Tommy's puddingy face seemed to look just then. It was the humble recognition of an unaccountable power, and he was trusting to it, as we do well to trust those glittering things when any such powers come near us. And that trust and the imminence of that power transformed his face, till the rather vacant smile was drawn to a narrower feature and the unintelligent eyes were awed to a sombre gaze. It was like this that Lily mostly knew him; it was thus that he looked as he blew those bursts of unearthly music, and thus she had seen him gaze from

Wold Hill into the darkness as though at things inscrutable to her, as though there were some dim secret that he shared alone with Fate.

Strangely unlike was this lad that she knew on the hill to the Tommy Duffin that they knew in the village; and more than ever now was this strange unlikeness manifest, so that the eager pensive face that was close to hers was scarce to be recognised even in a better light for the uninspired red face that his father and mother knew.

And gradually Tommy's blind faith in his strange power spread its influence over Lily, till both were trusting in a force of which neither knew anything, which had come to one of them from they knew not where.

13
The Original Language

Whatever vacillations[1] Anwrel had shown he resolutely held to his main purpose. The attitude that the Bishop had taken had been to the vicar like some sheer cliff, met suddenly by a hunter on his way through tropical forests: he tries to climb it and cannot; he goes to the left and comes back and tries to the right: but however often he hesitate before that sudden ending to every path he does not for an instant abandon his quest, but holds on till he finds some cleft of river or earthquake opening for him a way, and so comes through to achieve whatever it is that a fancy afire[2] in his blood has been urging him onward to do. And as the feet of the hunter pass down new tracks, so Anwrel's thoughts followed on from fact to fact: they scarcely ever ceased but were travelling always toward the clear light of reason that Anwrel felt sure must lie beyond all this mystery. It was clear that the Duffins were untroubled by anything dreadful overhanging them or menacing their posterity, and yet amongst their memories might well be found, unregarded

[1] Indecisions.
[2] Burning.

in all the lumber of the past, the very thing for which the vicar sought. So in the morning after the day of his sudden return from Snichester he left his house, for the third time seeking the Duffins. And, having no excuse for calling on them again so soon after his last visit, he went by a footpath that led by the side of Duffin's best hayfield, believing that if he walked slowly he was sure to see the farmer, either as he went or returned, going to look at the ripening of his hay; for it drew near to the season of haymaking. And sure enough he soon found him, gazing over his hay, his face full of anxiety.

"You've a fine crop there," called the vicar.

"Aye, sir," said Duffin, coming toward the footpath. "A thunderstorm any time this week will lay it flat."

"But we're having glorious weather," said the vicar. "Glorious."

"It's the hot weather that brings the thunderstorms, sir," Duffin replied.

Duffin was no croaker,[3] but the hay was exceptionally good, further on by some days than he had ever known it, and the approaching wealth seemed to come with clouds of anxieties. These anxieties Anwrel could have brushed away, as he had done with so many during his years in Wolding, but his cheery spirit was weighted too much with his own, and with one of those jerks unusual in conversation he went straight to the matter in hand.

"About your boy, Duffin," he said.

"Yes, sir," said Duffin, "he's been giving a lot of trouble of late."

"If it isn't entirely his fault," the vicar answered. "If there should be any influence affecting him of which we know nothing. Why, then we shouldn't be too hard on him, should we?"

"Oh, it isn't nothing of that, sir," said Duffin.

"But the past, you know," said the vicar. "All sorts of things come out of the past. More than we think. And they're very

---

[3] In this context, a person who habitually predicts evil.

ch. ends p. 70

strong, some of them. If there was anything influencing a man from a long way back, it might have a terrible hold on him. One never knows."

"Oh, there's nothing of that sort affecting Tommy," was all Duffin said.

"Now can you remember," the vicar asked, "if the Reverend Arthur Davidson ever came to this house?"

"Him, sir," said Duffin. "No, never."

"Ah," said the vicar. "Then did you see much of him at any time, anywhere else?"

"Only in church, sir," said the mystified Duffin.

"Only in church," urged the vicar. "You're quite sure?"

"Sure as I can be, sir. But what has him to do with Tommy?"

"You're quite sure — you know the kind of man they say he was — you're quite sure he never at any time laid any curse on you or on this house. Nothing of that sort ever happened so far as you know?"

"A curse, sir?" said Duffin. "A curse? What should he do that for?"

"Well, you know the sort of things they say of him," answered the vicar. "You knew him. You'd know better than me."

"What sort of things?" asked Duffin.

"That he mightn't stop short of doing a thing like that," the vicar replied.

"Well, yes, sir," Duffin admitted. "I have heard that sort of talk. But he'd never have done such a thing as that. Would he, sir?"

"He doesn't seem to have been quite what he appeared," was all the vicar said.

"Well, he never had a chance of doing it as far as I know, sir," said Duffin. "But that couldn't have affected Tommy, could it, sir?"

"You never know with a curse," said the vicar.

"Ah, that's where it is," said Duffin. "We don't even know if there are such things."

"Then I may take it you are quite sure he never had any opportunity of putting any sort of curse upon either of you."

"Not unless he did it to a score[4] or so of other people at the same time," said Duffin, "for we never saw him except in church. I heard him read our banns[5] a few times. And very soon he left."

"And then, of course, he married you," said the vicar.

"Oh, yes, he married us, sir," said Duffin, and added, "I shall never forget that service."

"Yes, it's a beautiful service," said the vicar.

"It wasn't the service I meant, sir," Duffin replied. "It was when he spoke to us at the end in the original language."

"The original language?" said the vicar.

"That's what they said it must be, sir. He suddenly lifted his voice at the end of the service and said those beautiful words. You should have heard them, sir."

"But what words?" asked Anwrel.

"Ah, that I don't know, sir: they was all foreign. But you should have heard them, sir; you should indeed. There came a ring in his voice and he spoke to the missus and me, and he said those words same as if they were his own language, as though he loved them. They got you by the heart; they did indeed."

"But what did they sound like?"

"Ah, you should ask the missus that," said Duffin. "She used to remember them. She used to sing them. You couldn't say them quite: they was all music. But she sang them many a time the first year we was married. She'd sit and sing them at evening, all in the original language, not knowing a word of what any one of them meant. I used to think the world of her singing in those days. I thought the whole world of it. But I knew even then that she couldn't touch the Reverend Davidson. Oh, the voice he had."

"The curse!" exclaimed Anwrel.

---

[4] A score is twenty (20).

[5] A formal declaration on three successive Sundays in a parish church, announcing an intended marriage and giving the opportunity for objections.

ch. ends next p.

"It wasn't no curse, sir," said Duffin.

"I fear it," said the vicar.

So silent the vicar stood, amongst grave thoughts, that the farmer said never a word; and so the two men stayed for many long moments.

"Duffin," said the vicar at last, "we are law-abiding men. We must stick to the law whatever it is."

"Oh, yes, sir," said Duffin.

"And if there is anything in all this," said the vicar, "in any way touching on witchcraft, you know there are laws against that still on the statute-book. Magistrates are still sworn to punish it when they first take their oath. New or old, it's the law, and we must abide by it, Duffin. If there's anything of that sort wrong with Tommy, it's the duty of all of us to put a stop to it."

And at last a clear way showed to the farmer out of all these strange perplexities into which the vicar was leading him.

"Whatever it is, sir," he said, "that young Tommy is up to there'll be an end to it all this evening."

"An end to it?" said the vicar, with a feeling, about his heart, of a burden shifting, such a feeling as Alpine slopes may have in Spring before the avalanche leaves them.

"An end to it, sir," said Duffin.

The Gathering About the Fire

And, even as Duffin and the vicar talked, the plan that Duffin knew of was holding a little circle of young men like a spell. On the slope of the hill, not far from Valley Farm, they were gathered about a fire under a hedge, some seated, some standing, all carrying sticks, ten or a dozen lads about Tommy's age that had gone up there to be alone with their plan. The object of the fire, they said, was to cook their food in case they should be out there a long time; but the serious business of that fire was to give a touch of mystery to their project, and to link them with all adventurers that had ever set out from comfortable homes and had gone to the hills to hunt man. For these lads that the fire united, and welded into a band, were hunting Tommy Duffin. Each one had reason enough to join that band that was gathered now about the fire of sticks, planning to stop the pipes, for each had brooded about Tommy Duffin often in lonely evenings; at first denying that he had any strange power, then jealous that such a power should ever have come to him, perhaps feeling that, when it had come so near themselves, it passed only by blind injustice to Tommy Duffin; and the loneliness of the long evenings had made the broodings bitterer. Each one had grievance enough. And yet when they spoke by the fire it was not of this. For the little group by the fire took no heed of personal grievance: the old ways were in danger; something strange had come and was threatening the old ways, and they were gathered there to defend the things they knew, the old familiar ways that were threatened now by this tune that troubled the evenings. They thought of the days when this had never been, when none went to the hill at dusk, and no strange longings arose to draw them westward, and there was nothing to puzzle them; and as they thought of these days they seemed the best, and they swore they should be again. And so they planned to come on Tommy Duffin at once, and to catch him that evening and to take away his pipes, and so make an end of the longings that haunted the hill. Already they had watched him at evening and knew his habits, knew by what path he would steal away to the hill, and when to expect his coming, as the hunter in wild lands knows the hour of his quarry. And now each lad by the fire had his place appointed to him by their leader, Willie Latten. A hedge went up from the village right up Wold Hill: to the left of it men ploughed and sowed the slope, but to the right it was all wild hill, too steep to plough, and it was here that young Duffin used to come with his pipes, playing among the wild-rose trees. Five of them were to go along this hedge as soon as they heard the pipes; and, keeping on the side of the tended fields, were to get as near as they could to Tommy Duffin without letting him see them. Three more of them were to come straight up the hill, more to the right, below where Tommy Duffin would be; using what cover there was, and getting as near as they could without being seen by the piper or by the girls that usually sat there a little below him. And away on the right three more were to come by the clematis lane, past the little house in which Lily was parlourmaid; then spreading out over the hill. As soon as Tommy Duffin saw any one of them all the rest were to close in. They knew which way he would go. They had seen him take alarm in the dusk before. He would go up the hill through the woods, and away toward the other side where the old stones were; and they would have half a dozen lads in the wood behind him, and more if they could find them by evening. There would be no escape for Tommy Duffin. These were the plans of the band of lads by the fire, the orders of Willie Latten; and they were received by the rest as by an army, and a band of conspirators, and knights pledged to a quest, for somehow romance rose up in the smoke of the wood-fire and blessed them. But, however much anything fanciful had come to them out of the past, their plans were sufficiently practical: romance was the inspiration of their project, but practical common sense went to the carrying out of it, a very potent alliance. None who knows the hill on which Tommy Duffin used to play his pipes of reed will doubt that by this plan he would be as completely surrounded as might be.

They scattered then, leaving one to quench the fire; and all went back by different ways to the village, every one of them hushed and delighted by the burden of their great secret. And little they spoke all day at their work on the farms, for their thoughts were away with their plan on the slope of Wold Hill at sunset.

And the day passed, as even years will pass, and the long shadows came stalking down from the hill; and Willie Latten's band of young men slipped away from their homes, with that altered air about every one that there is on a dog going poaching. Their gathering-place was the circle of grey ash where their fire had been in the morning. They had brought paper and matches to light it again and were gathering bits of old bramble, when Willie Latten stopped them. There must be no fire, he said: the smoke would be seen over the hedge by Duffin. This disappointed the rest, but the secrecy of the precaution appealed to their sense of mystery, and seemed to bring everything for which they waited much nearer. From this gathering-place Willie Latten sent off at once the six that were to wait in the wood on the top of the hill, between Tommy Duffin and the Old Stones of Wolding. They went up the hill

ch. ends next p.

along the side of the hedge, all stooping so as to be completely hidden from anyone on the wild part of the slope. And with them went the three that were to come from the clematis lane: for the lane just touched the very end of the wood before sending an open path to straggle on over the grassy slope; and they could reach it unseen by going through the wood all along the top of the hill. When these had gone Willie Latten sent down to the village the three that were to come up from below after Duffin had come to the hill, telling them to hang about by the back of the forge until he gave them the signal. Then leaving by the ashes of the old fire the three that were to come along the hill from the South he went down into the valley himself, to watch young Duffin's movements; and there were few in the village, young or old, who could watch without being seen like Willie Latten.

15
They Come to the Old Stones

On that day just after sunset Tommy Duffin left Valley Farm, going quietly out of the house and loitering away, only quickening his pace as soon as he was out of sight of the windows. He went swiftly and furtively, avoiding roads and open spaces, preferring hedges and shadows, like a fox at the edge of the woods; but whenever anyone saw him he dropped at once into a certain aimless gait, as though he were one with listless formal folk, returning as soon as their eyes were off him to his purposeful prowl again. So he passed along the outskirts of the village, and often he passed unseen. But today some wisdom he seemed to share with the wild, some lore that is known to the creatures dwelling apart from man, was hinting again and again to him that he was followed. He stopped and looked round: nothing was stirring behind him, but still that feeling that he was being watched. So he went on; then stopped and turned suddenly. And still he saw nothing. And still the strange wisdom warned him.

When he tried a third time and yet could see no watcher, he ignored the wisdom though he could not forget it; and went on, and came to Wold Hill, and climbed it until the wild slope was all about him with its briar and thorn and long grasses; and all the wild roses seemed to welcome him. He sat down then where a low briar-rose just hid him from the windows of Wolding, and turning first toward the house that stood out of sight behind the waves of wild clematis he put his pipes to his lips and played one call. The clear call came to the house and made Lily gasp, and the old woman wondered again; and the vicar heard it and sighed; and it passed right over the village bringing its tumult of thoughts, and it wandered away through the air till it grew so faint that it only stirred strange fancies in minds that were not aware that the notes had come to their hearing. Lily put down a tray that she had in her hands and came quietly away at once. Mrs. Airland said nothing now: she had some while ceased to do more about that wonderful music that we do about meteorites. The vicar sighed again. Down in the village their thoughts went wandering awhile to far times and curious rites. Girls stole away up the hill. And there came a thrill to the band of Willie Latten, as when an army hears a foreign trumpet blowing a call toward them that they have not heard before. He blew another call and the girls came running. Then with Lily beside him, and the rest seated near, a crescent of young girls among the wild roses, Tommy Duffin softly played a tune on his pipes that was like the sound of young streams running fresh from small mountains, heard in dreams or imagination, with birds fluting along the banks on some wonderful morning that are none of the birds we know, or ever shall. So faint was the tune that held those girls wondering, so magical and so new, that when a gust of it ceased, it seemed all to have been but a dream, such as comes and passes in the moment of waking upon some radiant morning; and nothing remained to show that it had been real but the darkened pupils of the wondering eyes of the thrilled girls that had listened.

Again he blew on the pipes; a tune like the voices of blackbirds heard from far valleys, telling over among themselves some happy tale too light and wild for any affair of man; from far, far valleys, too far to come to our hearing, and only reaching us through memory, where such things are stored far back amongst dust of our earliest years. As that rapt audience sat still as briar and thorn the three young men that were to come from below began to move up the hill.

Suddenly Lily saw them. She sprang up and screamed to Tommy. All the other girls rose and looked round angrily, staring at those three men as though they thought some of Medusa's power were theirs.[1] Then they saw the others from the clematis lane, and soon some more on their left: they stood irresolute then. And Willie Latten's young men closed in as he had planned. Tommy had risen too, and was standing with his pipes in his hand hanging down at his right side, while Lily was clutching at his other arm trying to drag him away. But Tommy was standing like a man in thought, though he was not thinking, but he seemed unconscious of Lily or any around him, while, with head lifted in stillness he let some influence from the hills pour into his heart.

It was not till the men were quite close that Lily realised she could not move him; then she stood still and gazed at Tommy, knowing it was too late for anything she could do, and falling back on her trust in him as the only hope she had; and all the other girls stood still and uncertain. The men had come softly enough at first, but they were all hurrying now. And then Tommy Duffin raised his pipes again, and blew clear on them when all the men were close. And at the first bar of that music something came over Willie Latten's men that was quite new to them, and their thoughts went wandering away to it, and would have stayed awhile, for it was so strange; then they put it away and came on a little further. But now some mystery from beyond the hills and out of old ages had surely beckoned to them, and had something to say; and they paused then, feeling they must hear it. Now all the slope was ringing loud with the music. They gazed round as though to see from what part of

---

[1] In Greek mythology, Medusa is generally described as a woman with living snakes in place of hair whose appearance was so hideous that anyone who looked upon her was turned to stone.

ch. ends next p.

the circle of hills that hidden thing had come near. Still they saw nothing: still they felt that something had come out of the deeps of the twilight and moved nearer to them along the notes of Tommy Duffin's pipes. And suddenly they knew that the mystery of the hills, and the deep enchantment of evening, had found a voice and would speak with them. They stood very still then, and listened. And their thoughts went far from their gathering by the fire, and far from Tommy Duffin, and went roaming away to memories so remote that they passed those gates that we commonly name forgetfulness, to remember things that their great-great grandfathers knew, old tales carried over the years by legend awhile, and dropped at last till the grave believed it had harvested all. These ancient things they remembered, standing there, with the evening all around them full of a meaning it had barely hinted before. All were stock still and silent, girls and boys, all but Tommy Duffin pouring out the notes of that inspiration that passed by him on its way from unknown to unknown. He paused, and turned in the hush, his face now to the rising slope and the black of the woods. And then he played a time that was utterly new to him, and strode away up the hill. They looked to each other to ask if they should follow: none gave the word, none spoke. All followed. It was not strange that they followed; for the new tune that Tommy Duffin was playing was the march of the things of the wild. There were calls in it that are known to birds that migrate, which their leaders utter at the turn of the wind that shall carry them on their journey; there were notes that were taken from the quavering ending of howls that have summoned packs; there were notes of earthly trumpets and, following after, clear answers from elfin horns. All manner of tides of life had moved to the notes of that music; it was no wonder they followed.

And following Tommy Duffin they came to the dark wood; and the pipes set its nooks and hollows astir with a sudden magic. The lads that waited for him in the wood heard that magic coming nearer: it seemed as if all the mystery that lurked among aged trees had suddenly stirred from its sleep, and were calling to them aloud after so long a silence. Nearer it came till the very bracken all round them rang with its wonder. They forgot their quest, they forgot the plans by the fire; the wood was full of the voices of old magics, all echoing with tales of far away, all echoing with a wonder and a beauty such as no tales had had since they were very young. They rose as the piper went by them, standing voiceless and still; and after him they went away through the wood. And he and all that little following went up the slope over the gnarled old beech-roots, and over the crest and down through the dark of the pines, till the single trunks stood out before them, each against fading sky. And so the piper led them all through the wood, till they came to the valley beyond, where the Old Stones lay in a field, dark shapes in the dimness of evening.

When Tommy Duffin saw the Old Stones of Wolding he knew why he had come that way, knew then that ancient rites about those old stones were luring him back to them from right across Wold Hill and from ages and ages ago. Then he blew a tune that the pen cannot keep pace with, that words cannot overtake, yet it spoke to his little following with strange word-less meanings. The time was now like a wind blowing over the downs at night, and blowing over the ages, a shrill sad wind with a voice too laden with wisdom for words. It seemed to hold for them some ancient secret, so that curiosity alone would have drawn them if there were no other force; but an awe and a holiness were welling up from the tune and blessing the old dark stones, so that they could not draw back from them, and all the while the music was lifting and lifting their feet, and their reason was long since lulled and was all asleep. So they came to the tune of pipes to the Old Stones of Wolding.

They Dance to the Pipes of Reed

The vicar in his study had listened to those clear notes going over the hill so wildly. He had listened with hearing sharpened by the long strain of worry, and had waited for the wild music to come to a sudden end; but it had merely faded away, going on to haunt further valleys, as he feared only too rightly. They had listened, too, in the village: they could not choose but listen. And as portentous[1] things are noticed in stirring times, when the upheavals of Nature or war force strange changes upon the notice of those that look for no changes, so they noticed now that neither in streets nor houses were there any young men or girls. For long enough they had known that something strange was afoot, for long enough they had mistrusted that music, and doubted their daughters when they told them where they had gone late in the long evenings; but their lives for some while now had been lived according to reason and by the light of queer old traditions, and the effort to recognise that there was something amongst them now, that had nothing to do with reason or any tradition they knew, was too much for them till it

[1] Foreboding; ominous.

came and stared in their faces. And it was staring them in their faces now. There were no young men in the street, no girls in the houses, and that music was haunting the hill, and its echoes drifting like ghosts of an unknown people up and down their familiar streets and below the eaves of their houses. And while they wondered and guessed, something more strange than their wonder and far afield of their guesses was taking place on the other side of the wood whose blackness now darkened Wolding. For when Tommy Duffin came to the Old Stones he changed his tune again, and began to dance round the circle, weaving the steps of his dance in and out of the old stones, inside one, outside the next, till he had gone round all twelve. This he did three times, and they all followed. And the steps of their dance came easy, though they had known none like it before; and the tune seemed some melody they had known of old, before some change had come which they could not remember. And a great planet came shining out like silver, and all the stars appeared. Then Tommy Duffin went to the long flat stone that lay in the midst of the circle, and stood by it piping, and they all danced on and on. And then he drew them all past the central stone; for, so strong was the grip of the music, he was able to do that; and they all came by and bowed to the flat stone as they passed it. Nobody thought to bow, and none questioned why he had done it: it had been the thing to bow to the old flat stone far back in the dark of time, and somehow the music was lighting up the ways of that bygone day. And, as the tune drew gradually down the ages the ritual to which the Old Stones were accustomed once, wilder dances and stranger rites came back to that valley after so long a while, for the music disturbed the heavy sleep of oblivion that history could not stir. So there danced about those old, remembering stones, this way and that way as the strange music swept them, like fallen leaves on varying gusts of wind, Willie Latten and all his men, who had thought to break the pipes with a twist of the hand; and with them went the girls they had planned to free; for there was in the pipes a power that drew to the Old Stones, as in

ch. ends next p.

Summer the North draws swallows.[2] The eyes of the beasts in the wood peered out and saw them; light breezes touched them that go down valleys at night, unfelt, unknown by men, upon secret errands of nature, carrying pollen for flowers, floating green-eyed moths on their journeys: all the whispering things of the night were about them now. And nearer, it seemed, than ever they were before; as though the fear of man, with which he has clothed himself in the course of the centuries, with all his speed and his noise, were thrown away when he went to the Old Stones.

They rested awhile, the pipes playing softly on, and all the tides of night flowed over them; winds, and the scent of flowers, a white owl floating by, the particular tribe of moths whose hour it was, and the imperceptible march of all the stars. And tired though they were with dancing, and full as they were with the wonder that haunted the night, the magic of those reed pipes and the mystery of the Old Stones, yet still they felt there was something more to be done. And they gazed at the long flat stone, looking anxiously at it, all fixing their eyes on its grey shape seen by starlight. At last Willie Latten spoke, voicing what they all felt.

"It has an empty look, the old flat stone."

"An empty look," they all said.

They were thinking of sacrifices such as reddened old stones in times of which none had taught them.

And the pipes went on and on with their low monotony, calling up such memories as these, that were lying deep in the ages, and that came as rarely to the light of our day as the soft white things that lived under the silent stones.

"An empty look," they repeated.

And Willie Latten's men began muttering of sacrifice. One hinted a sheep, in tones hushed by the awe of the long stone. "It should be a bull," said another.

And the little band that had gathered to break the pipes

---

[2] Migratory swift-flying songbirds with a forked tails and long pointed wings.

and to overcome the strangeness they brought to Wolding, planned now whose bull they should take for the long flat stone. And most were for going at once, and getting a bull that they all knew where to find, and leading him up and sacrificing him there to the dim immortals they knew not, on the long flat stone in the dark when none could see what they did. Till Willie Latten, speaking loudly and clearly above their hushed debating, said: "That's not the time to sacrifice a bull."

And each one felt in his heart that it should be done at dawn.

But this they could not do, when the world was awake. They could even be seen from a road. Thus they spoke in low tones awhile, the future more full of mystery than they had ever felt it before.

Then they danced again to the skirl of the reed pipes, that rose slowly loud out of the murmuring notes that were only hinting strange tunes; and louder still they grew and stranger still, till it almost felt as though some hidden piper, of no mortal fabric, but made out of hills and woods, lurked behind Tommy Duffin.

And suddenly a splendour seemed to go out of the stars, as though they could not hold the night much longer. And at that the dancers slipped away through the wood, while the pipes sent a softer air through the fading night, and Lily crept alone to the long flat stone.

Now there had been no paganism in Wolding since St. Ethelbruda's time.

17

The March of the Old Folk

In the hint of light before dawn, in the darkness of night, the lads and girls that had danced came back to the village before even one early candle gilded a window, before any birds were astir. And the houses to which they came were stiller than night itself, seeming among all the sounds that strayed in the dark of the valley to stand as chilling monuments to silence. Within them creaks and echoes seemed to rise up all together, in protest against the intrusion upon this hour; but no one in any house waited up so late, and those that returned all reached their beds unseen. Then all the blackbirds burst into sudden song.

But when the morning came that the birds had foretold, and grew broad and awakened men, then none that had danced escaped questions; and few could give answers that appeased their elders at all. There is always a gap between the generations: the old have forgotten so much and the young have yet to learn. Sometimes quiet ages pass, and nothing pushes aside the little bridges that custom throws across time from one to the next generation: sometimes come ages when tumultuous changes widen all the gaps, and the little bridges fall in. Such a change was come now, not to the age, which was little concerned with that out-of-the-way valley, but to the little village of Wolding.

At first there had only gone to the hill to hear the strange music girls, I will not say young enough for romance, for that may hold them long after rheumatism has settled in for good, but young enough to act upon it; and now there had gone the lads that were young enough to look for a fight and to make their plans by a campfire. None of the older folk had gone by night to the hill to hear the pipes playing; and now with their thoughts on the village and the quiet ways that had made it, and the orderly thoughts that ruled it, and the old folk that had left it, and the tales that had gathered about it like clambering plants over porches, they questioned those whose thoughts were away with the voices of night, with a small wind whispering to branches, with the wild things of the wood, and with a melody ringing clear down the ages so far that it touched the sleep of the Old Stones of Wolding, and received from their ancient silence an answer it understood. The gap between generations had widened all of a sudden.

Nor were the older folk ignorant, as their children supposed. They too had heard the pipes, they too had felt a strange lure in them; but what they guessed was too wild and too fantastic, above all too madly at variance with the way of life to which they had long settled, and so they put the guess deliberately away; soberly, rationally and rightly, as they would have said themselves; and so it remained a suspicion to excite them but was not knowledge to guide them. By the light of this suspicion they were all questioning their children.

That was the situation that was troubling Wolding that day. Knots of young men, all come from cheerless homes, gathered now and then to discuss in low voices what should be done. But even Willie Latten had no plan. It was one thing to plan with an excitement before him, which between them all with campfire and secrecy they had worked up into an adventure; but it was another thing to be the leader of a romantic band again, after

ch. ends p. 90

all he endured that morning, when all his poor excuses one by one were forced to unequal battle against logic.

"Lily," said Mrs. Airland. "I thought I missed you last evening."

"Did you, Mum?" said Lily.

But there was a light in Lily's eyes, like a strong sword suddenly drawn, and all at once Mrs. Airland felt too old to fight out the battle of words she had just begun.

In every other house the girls that had danced drank deep of the misery of that morning.

So little groups stood in the village street reluctant to go home, telling each other their troubles, their arguments and resentments; and all the while there rose up over them all a feeling as of something about to happen, as though something hidden in the dark of the future, and rushing nearer on the current of Time, oppressed the village with its threatened arrival. Such feelings come to nerves jangled and hearts troubled, and are often no less true than things that are known to hearts not stirred from their natural quiet. For those that went home at the dinner-hour it all began again. And now the afternoon was wearing away, and the white street left so often at this hour alone with the sunlight, and perhaps one donkey rolling in the warm dust, was now all ill at ease; for the quiet of the slanting rays, soft dust and the green of the hill was somehow stirred from its benignant rest by the trouble and irritation of the young men loitering there.

Tommy Duffin was not in sight and the others spoke of him seldom, because in this trouble that was raging in Wolding between the generations each had his own wrongs and own apprehensions, which seemed matter enough for discussion: no more seemed needed. And if ever his name were mentioned, the same phrase came like its echo: "Tommy Duffin's catching it." For they supposed him to be still at Valley Farm, enduring what they had endured.

Through the quiet of this evening and its vibrating troubles came a man walking calmly, a contrast to the querulousness[1] of the young men and their excitement, a dark figure walking the road that came across the valley: placidly enough he approached, though his eyes were somehow troubled; and they saw it was Anwrel. He called out to none, nor seemed to approach them with any desire to speak; he merely watched them as he trod the road slowly. And here, though he never spoke, they recognised the reproof of the generation on the other side of the gulf from them. As he passed the groups of young men they touched their hats, and he gravely raised a hand to his own broad brim, but he said never a word. Slow though he made his pace he could not have been in their sight for more than a few minutes; and yet they felt his reproof was chilling time and freezing the flight of the moments, and that the mild eyes of the vicar would blame them ever. They knew not how to excuse themselves.

Yet the strain of those minutes told more heavily upon Anwrel than on any of those young men. He seemed more lonely, more the antagonist of some portentous thing, that, dim though it was, had for him certain outlines of awful clearness, and it seemed that he must fight it quite alone. Yesterday he had hoped after speaking to Farmer Duffin, and had relaxed his resistance to a multitude of anxieties; and then had come that music overnight, and information enough the morning after, enough and to spare, and his anxieties had rushed back on him weakened by his few hours of hope, like raiders coming by night upon soldiers asleep. He hated no man: he could truthfully say that. Yet walking slowly there, with head bent, in that strained silence, his very presence a protest against those that should be his friends, young men of his loved parish, boys he had taught to bat, he felt an anger rising against Tommy Duffin who had worked all this confusion, an anger swelling and coming near to the thorny borders of hatred.

A woman opened a green door, showing a glimpse of a room,

---

[1] A complaining, petulant, or whining manner.

and called across the street to one of a group of young men: "Come here at once, Henry. You and your Tommy Duffin!"

He was not alone in his anger.

And then, then, there rose up out of the gold and the hush of the evening, a melody flooding the northern end of the hill, a music close at hand, but as remote from Anwrel's guesses as the literature of the interior of China, or a Lama's religion,[2] from ours. Once in a cathedral he had heard such music; not that time, but such music. It was long ago, before he had come to Wolding. He remembered the sanctity that filled the aisles, and had floated his feelings far from the fields of Earth: such emotions are felt once: when he went again the music eluded him. And yet it remained with him, gilding his memories, and filling a part of his mind with such traces of grandeur, as sunlight aslant through great windows, and a solemn dimness stirred almost to weeping or laughter by the tremendous traffic of those august echoes. And now, out here upon the open hillside, now music that once again had hold of his heartstrings, and the whole hill turned holy. Against such a feeling what could Anwrel do? He remembered Balaam on his high place, looking toward the Israelites, with Balak standing beside him bidding him curse.[3] So Anwrel felt his duty bidding him, but his heart would have blessed with Balaam. The hill seemed all holy, the tall dog-daisies[4] above the shining grass, the old deep hedge below and the woods above, haunted by dark yews, and the low and golden light in which it was all shining, right up to the shadows now creeping out from the wood.

And then came Tommy Duffin over the slope, playing his pipes of reed, playing like Apollo fresh from his golden home[5] and stirred by the first feel of the earthly grasses under and over his unsandalled feet. Not a word said the vicar.

---

[2] Dalai Lama; the title of a spiritual leader in Tibetan Buddhism.

[3] Numbers 23:13–24:25

[4] *Leucanthemum vulgare*; widespread grassland perennial wildflowers.

[5] In Greek and Roman Mythology, Apollo is the god of the sun, often described or portrayed in golden imagery.

A hush was now over the clusters of young men; over the whole street. A cock crew[6] a long way off; a dog barked and was silent. In the deep hush Tommy Duffin came to the road, and walked down the village street still playing his pipes. The young men turned as he passed, and followed in silence; two children playing looked up and followed too, a decorum suddenly still-ing their mirth and their leapings. And then a door opened, a green door of a small cottage, which somehow Anwrel remem-bered ever after, and a man appeared in the doorway, one older than Anwrel, standing very upright and stiff, with eyes fixed; he moved rather jerkily forward and joined the rest, and went down the village street after the music. And a woman, who had stayed to put a few things neatly away, came through the doorway after him. She came less uncouthly out of the little house than the man before her had come. She seemed going to something that comes by no choice of ours and is not to be criticized or resisted. However it be, she went; and kept pace with the younger steps, though with quicker breathing.

Another door opened, and quite an old woman came out of her house with a stick, old Mrs. Alkins whom one so seldom saw out-of-doors. She joined the rest, and another door opened and out came Mrs. Erceval, a widow this fifteen years; and then door after door. Skegland came out of his shop where one got the groceries ever since Anwrel could remember; then Latten, the carpenter, Willie Latten's father, and Mrs. Latten with him. And Hibbuts that had been sexton for the last thirty years, yes, Hibbuts, too.

It was the old people going, the quiet respectable folk, the very pillars of the little parish. Had Anwrel seen the painted wooden props, that held up the porches and were the homes of clematis, suddenly stride away, he would not have been more aghast.

And then, coming toward him from the house at the end of the hill, a lady like Mrs. Airland, only with a light in her face as

---

[6] Crowed; past tense of crow.

ch. ends next p.

though years had fallen away, with loneliness and fads and a touch of asthma; she came by him walking fast. Good gracious, it *was* Mrs. Airland.

The vicar stood there in the road, never speaking or moving, only staring after that departing procession. The sound of footsteps was fading, and a stillness settling over all the village, through which the notes of that music drifted yet. The sound seemed to turn to the right and go up the hill, and still the vicar stood listening. Why not go too? Why not go over the hill to the grey old stones, and hear that golden music beat against their ancient silence? There would be no perplexities amongst their calm, no weariness in the hold of that splendid music. Why not go too?

Yet if he went, who would stay? What would be left if he went? And in the end duty held him.

When that was decided the time had gone over the hill; and an old man stood alone, a little weary, very cold, and in tears.

18

Anything Might Come Up
Out of the Past

The light had gone out of the valley and off the hills when the vicar walked back through the village, as solitary a figure as you could imagine. Light still touched floating clouds, indeed the sky was full of it, but not a leaf flashed in Wolding, not a wall shone. It was a time of day when a man disappointed and troubled might brood long. And not a greeting came to lift Anwrel out of his broodings. They seemed all to have gone to the hill.

Through the village he went alone and came to his side of the valley, past the last silent house; when he saw a woman coming toward him, hurrying down the hill. One at least had not gone. Then he saw it was Mrs. Tichener. And he saw too that her hurrying was a simple and honest hurrying, to be home in her cottage before it got any later, with the packet of butter in paper that she was carrying. He hardly saw her until she was quite close, his eyes on the road and his thoughts in the midst of his broodings.

"Good evening, Mrs. Tichener," he said.

"Good evening, sir," said she. "I hope you're well, sir."

"Yes, yes, thank you," he answered.

He was always well. To him the question seemed scarcely worth asking. To her perhaps he looked a weary figure, barely convalescent after some illness or accident. Indeed he would have looked so to anyone that could have seen him then.

"Butter?" asked the vicar, pointing to the small white parcel.

"Yes, sir," she answered. "I've been up to Drover's to buy some. You never know what they put in it in the shops."

"You don't indeed," said the vicar.

She looked down the road, thinking how late it was growing. But the vicar did not move.

"Mrs. Tichener," he said after a while, "they're all going away after Tommy Duffin."

"With those pipes of his," she said thoughtfully.

"Yes," said the vicar. "There isn't a soul in the village."

"Aren't there, sir?" she said.

"Mrs. Tichener," he said, "what do you make of it?"

So direct an appeal moved her: perhaps the appeal was more in his voice than his words, or perhaps in his woe-begone face. Had it not moved her she would have lagged a little behind whatever the vicar said. Had he been mysterious she would have been less mysterious, had he turned toward wonder her words would have fared less far from the practical. For her mind was full of old tales and fabulous fancies, and all manner of little scraps of ancient wisdom, that had come to her from longer ago than the earliest tapestries in the oldest and luckiest families; and she knew that the vicar's education, that he had got when he was at Cambridge, was a light that could shrivel them up were they to be brought out to the glare of it. "Exposing her ignorance" was the phrase that she and her old friends would have been likely to use, had she told all she knew to the vicar. So there was a kind of shrine in her memory where she guarded things that had the appearance of being holy, and that might be a little ridiculous. But now a pity, where she suddenly saw the need of it, moved her to talk more freely, as emulation had moved her the day the vicar came back from Brighton.

"What do I make of it, sir?" she said. "Why I think it's that there Reverend Davidson."

"Yes," said the vicar thoughtfully.

"I think it's him all the time, sir."

"Yes. But how?" said the vicar.

"Well, sir," she said, "it's like this to me: there's an awful lot in the past; there must have been a dreadful lot of things happening that we've never heard about, since they first began. Well, sir, it's like something green coming bubbling up out of a deep well; you don't know where it's come from. Anything might come up out of the past like that."

"Good Lord," thought the vicar, driven homeward to Wolding by the metaphor, rather than carried out toward the infinite, "what awful water she must have been drinking."

"I hope you don't see things like that in your well," he said to her.

"Oh, the well's all right," she replied, "and so is the past, but anything might come up out of it."

"Yes, yes," the vicar muttered. "We can only see the surface, and a little way down of course. But do you think," he added louder, "that things like this could have come to us from the past?"

"Why, sir," she said, "you'd know more than me, with your learning and all that. I don't know what goings on they mayn't have had time for."

"Who?" said the vicar. "Whom do you mean?"

"Anybody, sir," she said, "in all the long time things have been happening."

"The Greeks had some such legend," he said. "But I thought it was all dead. I thought it was all dead."

She saw then that it was comfort he needed more than anything stored in her wisdom.

"But it will all sink back again one day, sir," she said. "It will all sink back."

He wished her good evening then, and went gravely on.

Night overtook the slow steps of the vicar as he went up the

ch. ends next p.

hill to his house, and he saw pale clouds streaming upward out of the East, and all the splendour of moonrise evident underneath them, though the woods and the hill upon his side of the valley would for some while hide from him any sight of the moon. He had come to mistrust such nights, not knowing how much the silver radiance with its faint touch of pale gold might inspire Tommy Duffin: he only knew that the moon had her ancient place in all pagan rites that he had heard of, and that it even presided over madness. He was therefore in no mood to admire the splendour of the light on the clouds from the moonrise, but only dreaded what fancies might come from it. Then he entered the house, and there was Augusta reading, a welcome sight, a new world to him. There at last was someone who would never go over that hill, never find any lure in that nonsensical music.

She looked up at him coming in so late.

"They have all gone over the hill with Tommy Duffin," he said.

"Have they?" she said quickly.

"Yes. It is very foolish of them," he said.

But she did not answer at once. "Yes. Yes, of course," she said then, looking straight in front of her.

And he knew it was no use saying to her things that he did not feel.

She too must have heard that music, but she did not speak of it.

Then he broke the silence by asking about their maid. "Is Marion here?" he said.

"No," she replied.

And he knew that Marion had gone away after the others.

Whether or not Mrs. Tweedy were gone he did not ask. They had cold supper in any case, so she might be still in the kitchen.

And the meal passed almost in silence. Augusta could not make light of it all now, as he had so much hoped she would; for he felt the need of being woken out of a dream that was too dark and much too long. But she could not do that after what she had heard; for the music had beaten across the valley, each note with a terrible clearness, and as full of a meaning, almost, as there is in words.

So Anwrel went to his study and lit his pipe, and sat there smoking late, and thought far back into time till he came to the slopes of Arcadia,[1] and tried to link old fables up with the things that were all about him, and saw thousands of pictures made by meditation amongst the smoke of his pipe, and yet saw no way out.

---

[1] A mountainous district in the Peloponnese of southern Greece. In Greek mythology it is the home of Pan.

19

The Tomb of St. Ethelbruda

A patch of moonlight shining bright on the wall awoke the vicar from dreams that were troubled by the sound of the pipes of reed. He listened then but heard no more of that music, and could not be sure if it came from the pipes or dreams. After that he slept no more, and soon dawn came. He dressed quietly then and stole away from the house, as though he fled from the thoughts that were troubling him; and climbed the hill and went through the still wood, and came out to the clear quiet light of the early morning. And certainly there far up on the airy hill, in that light and that freshness, thoughts that had loomed so large in the little room seemed smaller and weaker. And soon he was striding away with no moody step, over dewy grass and more cobwebs than one could credit, if one did not know the dawn. No reasoned plan directed his walk: first of all he felt he must leave a sleepless bed and walk in the still morning to think clearly, then the mood that brought him there directed his steps, and so he was going to the worn white stones said to be marble, that tradition named the tomb of St. Ethelbruda. Shaped like the sarcophagus of some crusader it stood right out in a field, with nothing to protect it from cattle but a few briars; and, as all Wolding believed, it cured warts.

When the vicar arrived at the worn white stones he stood a long while there. And soon he found he could reflect more calmly for being further from Wolding, for having come as it were from the enemy's lines to a friendly influence that was as a fortress against paganism. At any rate the sight of St. Ethelbruda's traditional resting place cheered him, and he at once thought more hopefully. First then he must have a long talk with Mrs. Tichener; he had been too downcast for that when he met her coming from Drover's: he must talk with her quietly about this thing that had come from the past; and when he had got to the bottom of that they would be able to find a remedy: with her help he could do wonders. And with the brightening of his mood the very morning brightened; which is not to be wondered at as the sun was climbing all the time; but Ethelbruda got some credit for it that we need not grudge to her.

Amongst seedlings of birches on slopes too steep to plough four different kinds of orchid were blooming where the vicar walked homeward through the splendid morning. When he returned his wife was down and breakfast was ready, which seemed very natural to him; but it was far too early for breakfast. Augusta seeing him gone had guessed a lonely walk, and certainly a hungry appetite; so everything was ready nearly an hour before its usual time. Hungry though he was he hurried, and soon he was off to the village to find Mrs. Tichener. He found her at breakfast.

"Mrs. Tichener," he said as he came in, "I want to have a long talk with you about Tommy Duffin and all this trouble he's making."

The cheerfulness died out of the end of his sentence as he saw the old woman's expression. For a sly look came over the face of Mrs. Tichener.

"Don't know very much about him, I'm afraid, sir," she said.

"No. But you had a theory about him," he said.

"Had I sir?" she replied.

ch. ends next p.

"About it all coming out of the past you know."

"Ah, but I know so little about the past," she said.

"It's not knowledge, exactly, that I want," he said. "It's more . . ."

But she interrupted him. "Won't you take a chair, sir?" she asked.

"Thank you. Another time. I must be going now," he said. "We'll have a talk some other day."

For he saw now it was hopeless. And he saw too that the music that had entered his dreams had been real music, though he always marvelled how a melody so fantastic could have any place in reality; for Mrs. Tichener had changed overnight, and must have followed the pipes to the old grey stones; and he was alone now in the village, the only enemy of that victorious music.

He walked home mournfully, thinking of his loneliness. Tomorrow would be Sunday; and he must prepare some sort of sermon with his distracted thoughts. He came back to the vicarage with no trace of the brightness he had got from the hills in the morning.

"Mrs. Tichener, too," was all he said to his wife. And she merely nodded with a little sigh. One has not need of many words in times of great disasters. He brooded some, while in silence; then raised his head as a brooding broke into words: "If only we weren't alone against it," he said.

"But you are not alone," she said.

"There's no one knows of it but us, that has not gone over to it," he answered.

"There's the man that took the service for you," she said, "when we were at Brighton."

He almost gasped; so greatly loom little things when they bear on a big trouble. He had forgotten him. He had forgotten all about him. The man had stayed three days at the vicarage and must have heard the music.

"Why, of course!" he exclaimed.

"His name was Hetley," she said.

"What? *The* Hetley?" asked Anwrel.

"I don't know anything else about him," she said, "but I know he was called Hetley."

"Did he come from near Snichester?" he asked.

"Yes, I believe so."

"But it's certainly *the* Hetley," he said. "Why. Fancy the Bishop sending him. It was really very good of him. The Bishop is going to help us after all!"

"Do you think so?" she said.

"Yes," said the vicar, "if he sends us a man like Hetley."

"What does he do?" she asked.

"Do," he replied. "Why, Hetley was one of the finest scholars at Gabriel's.[1] A Greek scholar, you know. A first-rate man. It was extremely kind of the Bishop."

"Do you know him?" she asked.

"Know him," he said. "No. I've seen him. I used to see him at Cambridge. But of course I don't know him."

It was unlike her to ask such a question: she should have understood that one didn't know men like Hetley. But she was urging her husband to go and see him. And when she suggested it, he said, "Why, yes, I must."

They knew where he lived, at Rolton;[2] so near to Snichester that the cathedral bells could be heard all over his parish.

And so they decided that he should go on Monday to meet this new ally. And the hope that he got from this sufficiently raised his spirits to face the weary task of preparing a sermon from which his thoughts were far distant. But as he sat in his study with his red ink and his black ink, and his sheet of foolscap before him, the old blue palaeolith that used to be but an ornament, seemed almost to leer at him with its wrinkles and hollows, as though the primitive were coming nearer and this old stone claimed some sort of equality with him now, to which it had never dared to presume before.

---

[1] Another Dunsany invention, used to evoke St. Gabriel, the archangel known for delivering divine messages.

[2] Yet another village of Dunsany's invention.

What Hetley Heard

It was a bright Sunday morning, and the Anwrels went down to the church for the morning service. To the few that they met on the way Anwrel said nothing. He saw a few entering the church, and one of the fears that had troubled him flew away. When the vicar came out of the vestry[1] he saw that the church was nearly as full as ever; and at that his hope increased, for he felt, whatever might come of it, that while the habit of coming to church was not overthrown his parish was invaded but not yet conquered. This feeling strengthened the high hopes he had from the conference he was to have with Hetley on Monday.

He preached to them much as he had ever preached, only without those little rises above his own level, that came every now and then, and that always surprised himself whenever they came. He made ample notes but did not write out his sermon, so that at any moment, he never knew when, there might come that ring in his voice, and some finer thought soaring up, above the rest of his theme. But none of these brief

---

[1] A room or building attached to a church, often used as an office and for changing into vestments (robes worn by the clergy during church services).

exaltations came today, for they come of an inner energy, and that had been all expended on thought and anxiety. He did not preach on the thing against which his heart and mind were struggling: he had thought of it overnight; and had got as far as looking up a text from where the children of Israel had worshipped the golden calf,[2] and, neater still, where all but three bowed down at the sound of the sackbut, psaltery, and all manner of instruments.[3] But in the end, still tired by the shock and anxiety, he did not feel he had strength enough to make this open attack on that goat-shaped enemy that was becoming more real to him than the personal Satan to the Salvation Army.[4] So he preached a sermon good and useful enough for any little parish, but drably contrasted with the strange event that had been stirring Wolding. And as he preached he noticed for the first time, although too slight to be sure about, a certain untidiness in his congregation.

When the service was over the vicar met his wife, as he always did, outside the vestry door; and, as always happened, he just fell in with the tail of his departing parishioners. This time it was Mr. and Mrs. Duffin. The vicar avoided their eyes and the Duffins avoided his, so that it might have seemed easy for them to go their separate ways. But the vicar felt that this avoidance was wrong, a sin of omission in a vicar, and called up a remark for Duffin, and a remark that, of all the remarks one might make, would be nearest to Duffin's heart.

"When are you going to cut your hay?" he said.

But Duffin brought back his thoughts as though from a distance.

"Oh, one of these days, sir," he said.

And it should have been the next day, for the hay was all ready to cut.

---

[2] Exodus 32

[3] Daniel 3:5

[4] Founded in 1865, The Salvation Army (TSA) is a Protestant Christian church and an international charitable organization headquartered in London, England.

ch. ends p. 104

"I am sure it will all come right," he said to Augusta on the way home, fortified by the fair attendance that there had been.

"Yes," she said. Yet something in her voice as she said the single syllable, or something in her eyes, seemed aware of a danger too great to be safely turned away from his thoughts for the sake of his peace of mind, as with a word or so she had often turned many anxieties.

"I will have a long talk about it with Mr. Hetley," he said. And he spoke as though talking to Hetley, let alone being answered by him, would solve great difficulties.

She was as anxious that he should see Hetley as combatant nations, in battle for their existence, are anxious for a new ally. Yet even there she could not or would not comfort him in such a way as to minimise the danger against which he was striving.

Somehow he knew that she felt more deeply than he; and, in spite of his more accurate information and greater knowledge, he continually looked to her opinion, as though any change in the situation would always be found there. And often during that day he asked her leading questions, all framed in the hope that her answer would brush the danger aside, so that his tired nerves could rest. And all the day, though she said little, it seemed as if, had she spoken, she would have uttered an icier fear of the end of it all, than he whose anxieties were so outspoken.

So that day passed with its shadows of dark forebodings; and Monday came that was to bring Anwrel a new ally, equipped with information from his actual visit to Wolding, and able to deal, if reputation goes for anything, with any human problem. Things all looked brighter that morning; and one small shadow was drifting from Anwrel's spirit, the shade of a trouble too little to bring a gloom, yet certainly casting a shadow, the refusal of help by the Bishop. That was what it had seemed to him, and thus it had been felt by his spirit, breeding an inner melancholy more deeply seated than will. And all the while the Bishop had sent Hetley, the ripest scholar of his year. He felt more grateful to the Bishop now than he would have if he had never suspected him of deserting him in his need. In the bright June morning, with an inner feeling that was brightening once again, he drove with Spelkins once more to Seldham station and took the train to Snichester.

There he arrived, and knowing the direction in which Rolton lay, walked straight over the fields to it.

Very soon he saw the trees rising over the hedges, both of which encircled the rectory[5] and church of Rolton. Great fields lay round it, stretching far away, and the trees seemed guarding that part of the parish from the level waste of the eternal fields. A few farmhouses straggled away behind.

He passed through the rampart[6] of trees by a wicket-gate in a hedge, and walked up a path to the rectory; and here he was calling on Hetley at the wrong time, and at the wrong door, for he had come to the door leading out to the lawns and the garden, and he could not find a bell. Hetley, however, who was writing downstairs in a room looking over the lawn, saw him at once and ran round to open the door.

Flustered apologies came from Anwrel first, at which Hetley smiled in a most friendly way, but said nothing. When they had come in and turned at once to their right they were in the room in which Hetley had been writing. The very appearance of Hetley encouraged him, scholarly but alert, a little grey; and a fine face still, if slightly weakened by time. Whatever was heard by this man would be somehow the more earthly for that; and Anwrel felt that his fears were to be called back at last from the infinite vast of phantasy[7] to the surer ground of the scholarly. What then had Hetley heard in his few days at Wolding? What had he made of it? These thoughts flashed past in a moment.

"My name is Anwrel," he said.

"Annel?" said Hetley.

"No, Anwrel."

"Oh, yes. I took the service for you at Wolding."

---

[5] The home of a rector, or priest.

[6] A defensive or protective wall-like barrier.

[7] Archaic spelling of fantasy.

ch. ends next p.

"It was most kind of you."

"I beg your pardon."

"I said it was most kind of you."

"Oh, don't mention it."

"I wanted to ask you," said Anwrel, "about what you heard when you were there. It's almost every evening. It's faint of course, yet every note of it marvellously clear. A music clear but not loud. You must have heard it."

"No," said the Rector. "I heard nothing."

21
The Wisdom of Hetley

The quiet remark that closed my last chapter brought an episode to an end like a cataclysm. We live more in hope than we think. And Anwrel had built so much on his hope of help from the Rector of Rolton that when that hope came to an end it was to him as tragic a loss as those greater mishaps that claim the attention of history.

And there was the Rector smiling at him across his table, near which Anwrel was seated in an armchair. He could not go immediately; and then came the thought to him that all was not yet lost, and that, though Hetley had no information with which to guide him, some help might be had from his learning. So he rallied all the forces of his mind, to save something from the forlorn situation, and speaking a little louder than he had spoken hitherto, began to question the Rector.

"I can remember you at Cambridge," he said.

"I remember seeing you at Gabriel's; though of course you wouldn't remember me."

"Yes, I think I do, I think I do," said Hetley. "You've changed a bit of course, but I think I remember your face. You were at . . ."

"At All Angels,"[1] said Anwrel.

"Yes, of course," said Hetley. "Yes, I remember you now. A long time ago. Wasn't it?"

"Yes," said Anwrel, "yes. I remember, of course we all remember, what a great Greek scholar you were."

"Oh, I was interested in it you know," said Hetley, "that was all."

"Ah," said Anwrel, "I have been interested, but without your knowledge that doesn't go for much. I have been particularly interested in one thing. You might perhaps care to tell me a little about it, only that it would be so unwarrantably taking up your time."

"Not in the very least," replied Hetley.

"I'm afraid I disturbed you when I broke in," said Anwrel with a look straight at the foolscap and ink-pot that were before Hetley.

"Not a bit," said Hetley, "I find relaxation as necessary for writing as ink. If you had not come in for a talk I should have gone out in another five minutes to dig up plantains.[2] Believe me: — I prefer a talk."

"It's awfully kind of you," said Anwrel. "Well, what I was interested in was how much their belief in Pan affected the lives of the Greeks. What rites they practised. What appearance they allege of Pan amongst them. Of course we all know the time he appeared to Phidippides.[3] But on what other occasions he came. And, and all that."

---

[1] "St. Michael and All Angels" is a common Anglican church name found throughout England.

[2] Not the banana cousin, but the *Plantago*—a genus of flowering plants in the Plantaginaceae family, commonly called plantains or fleaworts. Often seen as a lawn and garden nuisance, but has many medicinal uses.

[3] As per ancient Greek historian Herodotus, legendary Athenian runner Pheidippides, while en route to request Spartan aid before the Battle of Marathon in 490 BC, was crossing Mount Parthenium, in Arcadia, and claimed that Pan called out to him by name and asked why the Athenians had neglected him, and promised to help them again in the future. Believing Pheidippides, and once they had repelled the Persians at Marathon, the Athenians built a sanctuary beneath the Acropolis and began holding annual torch races and sacrifices in Pan's honor.

"Well," answered Hetley, "very few of those rites, or any really authentic appearance of Pan, seem to have come down to them past the Peloponnesian War,[4] which as you may possibly remember was where my period began."

"Your period began there?" said Anwrel so faintly that the Rector did not hear him.

"I beg your pardon," he said.

"You only began at the Peloponnesian War," Anwrel repeated.

"Yes," said Hetley, "I never studied earlier than that. It's a big period you know, the time of the Greeks. It's practically from the dawn of civilisation right up to broad morning."

"Oh, yes," Anwrel agreed.

"No, I never read anything earlier than the Peloponnesian War," said Hetley.

"And they worshipped Pan no more?" asked Anwrel.

"Well, they kept his fire alight for a while, perhaps for a hundred years. But ... "

"His fire?" said Anwrel.

"A fire on an altar that they had in a cave not far from the Acropolis.[5] But they let it out in a few generations."

"Then you think Pan never influenced them any later than that?" Anwrel asked.

"No, no," said Hetley, alarmed at being committed to any large statement he had not made, for he had a very considerable reputation. "I didn't say that. An influence is another matter. Of influences one may say that the more powerful the influence, whatever it is, the longer it will last. I can't say how long the influence came down, only that there seem to have been no authentic renewals of it in my period, the period I studied. They do not appear to have kept it alive themselves with any

[4] The war of 431–404 BC fought between Athens and Sparta with their respective allies. It ended in the total defeat of Athens and the transfer, for a brief period, of the leadership of Greece to Sparta.

[5] The Acropolis of Athens is an ancient citadel located on a rocky outcrop above the city of Athens, Greece, and contains the remains of several ancient buildings, the most famous being the Parthenon.

ch. ends next p.

important rites; and Pan himself does not appear to have . . . But I am speaking as though he really existed; one does sometimes speak from that point of view if one has been thoroughly immersed in the folklore of another age."

"Mr. Hetley," said Anwrel, "you never heard of the Reverend Arthur Davidson?"

"No," said Hetley, "I don't think I did."

"He did great harm in Wolding," said Anwrel, "before I came. In fact he absconded.[6] And I succeeded him. He did great harm there. And it is his influence, working now, *his* influence, that is turning my poor folk to the most heathen fancies. They still come to church, as you saw, but spiritually they are little better off than many that missionaries travel far to convert. And they are getting worse. They are getting worse."

"Well," said the Rector, "of course you preach to them. That is obvious. But if I may give a word of advice . . . "

"It is what I have come for," said Anwrel earnestly.

"You spoke of their spiritual needs," said Hetley. "I have always found that spiritual things follow very closely the physical. I remember being very much struck once by seeing some light white clouds over a range of hills; they took the shape of the hills exactly. What more ethereal than white clouds, what more material than rocky hills? And yet so it was. It was this chance observation that set me observing more; and I began to see in my own parish that boys that did not take exercise, boys who would not play games, were not merely less robust, which I had thought was the doctor's business, but were spiritually weaker and often had nasty minds, though they might be in the choir. It made me far more mundane. I had thought that the pulpit was my one strong place from which to attack sin, I now found a more impregnable place on the cricket-field. It was perhaps a humbling discovery, if I had credited myself with any learning, but having found it I held on to it."

"Yes; yes, I see," said Anwrel with a hopelessness in his tones that Hetley missed.

---

[6] Depart quickly and secretly to avoid punishment or prosecution.

"Yes, I got them fit, and keen on the game," continued Hetley. "It's a queer thing, but I can only give you the fact; they were much better choirboys. Now of course in cricket one must proceed intelligently, as in anything else; and, do you know, I found nobody all round me, teaching boys to play cricket, who ever taught them anything but batting. Sometimes perhaps they taught them to field as well, but that was all. Now just consider: supposing you have a team of boys that you've taught to bat: they can all bat a bit, but supposing you've taught them to bat a little bit better. What happens? They play another parish and make a lot of runs. Another day they play and make very few runs. Why? Simply because one parish had a bowler[7] and the other hadn't. A thing that everybody leaves merely to chance. But you can make bowlers."

"Yes, I see," said Anwrel mournfully.

But Hetley did not hear him.

"You can make them," he continued. "Choose a boy with long delicate fingers. Don't waste time with the others. And merely show him where to put those fingers. Why! There are boys who don't know what the seam of the ball is for. Tell them. And after that there is only one thing more. Pitch. Do you know what I give them to bowl at? A white handkerchief flat on the ground. If they knock the stumps down I leave them down. But if the handkerchief gets moved, back it goes at once. Pitch is everything. And if a boy can put five balls out of the six on to that handkerchief, he is a great bowler. Teach him to work his fingers on top of that, and he is invincible. Where are your village batsmen then? You get only one such boy on your team, and you'll win all your matches. You'll be able to do anything with your parish then."

"I fear it's too late," said Anwrel.

"Eh?"

"Too late."

---

[7] A bowler in cricket is similar to a pitcher in baseball.

22
Anwrel Looks at the Enemy

Anwrel left as soon as he could; shown out to the wicket-gate, the best stiles[1] and the readiest track pointed out to him, all with the utmost kindness; yet he left with more melancholy in his heart than I wish to tell, even if each vague trouble that harassed his thoughts could be reduced to coherent words. And equally vague were his hopes; for the cathedral was at first but a landmark to him, and the idea came only gradually to him to enter it, and therein to be assured, as he had been a week ago, that the conquest by Christianity was complete, and that so late in time as this, in these islands at any rate, there remained no enemy able to question it.

Logically, a fact in Wolding was a fact forever, and to look back at it from Snichester would not alter it. But distressed minds call on logic little more than men with broken legs send for the carpenter. The cathedral was growing enormous as he neared it, while Wolding was but a little thought in his mind, however vivid and painful. The cathedral with all the weight

[1] A series of steps or rungs in a wall or fence constructed so as to allow humans, but not animals, to pass over.

of material things, with all its vast bulk and its buttresses, imposed its point of view on all, far and wide over Snichester, and had done so, far through time. It was not merely a frail spiritual thing, like a poet's sonnet that the materialist could deride; it had weight and bulk and splendour. It was not easy to stand in those fields just where they lapped against Snichester, and to feel that the cathedral's cause had been defeated. So Anwrel found himself going toward the cathedral, as outposts worsted[2] in some little encounter fall back on a fortress.

One purpose he had in approaching it, as soon as that purpose grew clear, and that was to see in the vast fane[3] that all his fears were wrong: he wished a fact to become unenacted. And this illusion would have surely come to him amongst those quiet aisles, lit by dim light through pale windows and by the red glow through the dress of St. Ethelbruda. But coming to it by the way that he came, and not by the narrow street right underneath it by which he had come before, he looked upward more often, and saw far more of the great temple's exterior than he had ever thought about. It looked like a different land up there, raised up above our earth, a land of hills and valleys, with one great tower amongst them, and dozens of pinnacles; and even, as one came near, a white population, peering round high comers and over the tops of the walls, bright white like angels. He came nearer, still gazing upward. But they were not angels. As he walked slowly round the precipitous walls gazing up at the leering faces, all desire to enter the cathedral went; for among the things carved near the summit of that fortress of Christianity, among the things that Christian hands had fashioned, and that Christian minds must have known, was the very enemy that the Bishop would not fight, that Hetley would but half recognise, the conqueror of Wolding: goat-hooved Pan.

"You are looking at the gargoyles, sir?" said a verger,[4] coming up to that motionless figure gazing there.

---

[2] Defeated.

[3] Temple or shrine.

[4] A church official who serves as an attendant and caretaker.

ch. ends p. 115

"Yes," said Anwrel.

"That's Pan," said the verger.

"Yes."

The verger waited, ready to take him up the worn stone spiral staircase, to show him the gargoyles in which he seemed so interested. But Anwrel remained silent; till he said: "Do you think . . . ?" But did not complete his sentence and went away.

"Queer old bird," thought the verger, and went to find some-one else to take up to the roof to see his favourite gargoyles.

But Anwrel thought:— "They have known it. They have had this very thing in their consciousness. Christian men at work on a cathedral. And simple minds, not inventors or poets."

It made a world of difference. If he had feared, thought of, or seen, some fantastic thing that no one else had imagined, there was nothing in the telling of the story to separate it from the symptoms of delirium. But, terribly strange as was the experience that had befallen his parish, the actual influence came from a thing that no Christian had thought it strange to carve in stone, and that none were surprised to see whenever they went to attend the service in the cathedral. The Bishop could not say to him now, "What? Hooves did you say?" or "What! Reed pipes?" for the thing had been known for ages. He would go and see the Bishop.

So he went by curious houses, whose roofs the ages had undulated, by byways and narrow streets, and the bridge over the Snale,[5] and marched up to the Palace. He rang the bell resolutely; and, when the butler appeared, said: "Could I see the Bishop?"

"I will see, sir," said the butler, somehow conveying by his tones and his air that this most extravagant request would receive the kindliest consideration. And Anwrel was left with his thoughts, which were still resolute. He had been almost cowed by the awful loneliness of his disaster. Never had such a thing happened to any other parish. Never had anyone else's

---

[5] A river or stream of Dusany's invention.

imagination been burdened with the thing that burdened his. So he had felt till he saw Pan carved on the very cathedral wall. But now the loneliness at least had lifted: the thing had been known for ages. Dreadful it still was; but he would not have to explain it detail by detail to a doubting mind. It was known like murder, shocking, but credible enough. And, if anyone thought that the tale he told, as he had it from Mrs. Tichener, was a figment of delirium, he need only point to the cathedral.

The butler returned with the chaplain. He was dark-haired, very large, a bit younger than Anwrel, and very ruddy in the face.

"I am Anwrel from Wolding," said the vicar, "and I wanted to see the Bishop."

"Yes, yes, of course," said the chaplain.

"I'm afraid it's rather early to call, but . . . "

"Well, of course that *is* the trouble," said the chaplain. "The Bishop's very busy this morning. In fact he's receiving a deputation.[6] It's rather important, and may take some time. But if you would care to have a talk with me, I'm very much in with the Bishop's plans. And of course he has told me all about Wolding."

"All about it?" said Anwrel.

"Well, yes," said the chaplain. "You had a little trouble with some of your more frivolous parishioners I remember. My name's Porton. You know I wrote to you?"

"Yes," said Anwrel.

"But won't you come in here?" And the chaplain led the way to a room adjoining the hall. "We smoke in here. Will you have a cigar?"

Anwrel declined it.

"I'm sorry the Bishop won't be disengaged all the morning," said Porton, "but it's a rather important meeting. It's about those words, you know, in the National Anthem. Scatter his

---

[6] The appointment of a person or persons to represent or act on behalf of others or a larger group.

ch. ends next p.

enemies.[7] There's a widespread feeling that that is no Christian sentiment and cannot be reconciled with Christian feeling. The Liberal party are almost solid about it. And it is felt that either the words should be altered and the thing expressed far more mildly, or, better still, that the whole of that verse should be rewritten, by someone with a taste for writing verse, in such a manner as to give no offence to anybody, at home or abroad. I believe that will be done. Meanwhile the Bishop has to decide what recommendation should go up from this diocese."

"I see," said Anwrel.

"But you wished to talk about Wolding."

"Yes," said Anwrel.

"I hope you found those little lodgings all you could desire."

"Oh yes."

"And everything was all right when you got back to Wolding."

"Not quite."

"Not quite," said Porton. "Dear me."

"No," said Anwrel.

"And what was it that was not quite as it should be?"

"The way that they practise the rites of Pan instead of the Christian faith," Anwrel answered.

"Dear me," said the chaplain. "They shouldn't do that of course. Not at all. But are you quite sure it's as bad as that? Are you sure they really, that they really do?"

"You've heard of the Old Stones of Wolding. Something Druidic,[8] or earlier. Pagan at any rate. They do some sort of worship there."

The chaplain's method of getting through the great amount of business he had to do was to make everything as jolly as possible, and for this he was well adapted. But he did not look jovial now; his eyes looked a little frightened.

---

[7] "O Lord our God arise/Scatter his enemies/And make them fall" are lyrics to an additional stanza of "God Save the King," the national anthem of the United Kingdom.

[8] Druids were members of a high-ranking priestly class in ancient Celtic cultures.

"I think the Bishop will be able to see you in about an hour," he said. "Could you come back in an hour's time?"

"Oh yes," said Anwrel.

"And I should get them to play cricket as much as possible," said the chaplain. "Get them interested in that, and they'll give up any silliness with those stones."

"Very well. I will," said Anwrel.

23
The Woods of the Night

Anwrel went out into the street with a fear, now growing into a certainty, that a situation too terrible to be faced would be dealt with merely by never being admitted. Ways of escape seemed to lead away from it, mostly toward the cricket-ground. For others, but not for him. He began to see that those charged with administrative duties might, for all their skill, make nothing of such a situation. He greatly feared that they might refuse to admit it, turning away from it altogether, rather than risk their strength in a losing fight. But these fears that none would help him, and the assumption that Pan must win, came partly from an oversight of some importance in any difficulty: it was half past two and he had forgotten his lunch. This he remedied at The Green Man,[1] an inn that had never borrowed from French palaces the foreign name of hôtel, but called itself in honest English an inn; whose bow window on its first storey bulged out over the street, and where cold roast beef was ready. Here

[1] In his first autobiography, *Patches of Sunlight* (p. 62), Dunsany mentions bicycling into the village of Wymondham, in South Norfolk, to play chess at The Green Man.

he waited long, and pulled out his pipe and smoked after his meal, and thought with none to disturb him.

He was determined to persist in his demand for help, whatever the Bishop's attitude. What puritanical fire was it that urged him on to fight so resolutely against that music that had entered his heart with its wild appeal and its pagan inspirations as much as anybody else's in Wolding? Beautiful though it was, heart-soothing, and satisfying to yearnings that nothing else could appease, he knew it for the enemy and would not give in.

When it was time for him to return to the Palace he arrived at the door punctually.

"This way, sir," said the butler.

They came to a room in which the Bishop was sitting.

"Ah," said the Bishop after shaking hands, "my chaplain told me you had some difficulty in Wolding."

"Yes, my lord."

"I remember you writing to me. There was some music you heard sometimes, and not quite the kind of music that . . . well a fantastic kind of thing, that rather excites the mind than performs the true function of music, which is of course the exact opposite."

"Just so, my lord."

"Whoever plays it would be better occupied," said the Bishop.

"Yes, my lord; if I were able to persuade him."

"Exactly. And your own occupations? You have plenty of interests for light diversion in your leisure hours, which are no doubt few?"

"I collect flowers, my lord, at this time of year."

"Ah, yes. I have Sowerby here if you would ever like to look up anything."[2]

"I'm afraid," said Anwrel, "that mine is an entirely unscientific collection. What we do is, my wife and I, we have a bowl which we fill with orchids when they first come out, the twayblade and the helleborine. Then we get the spotted orchid and

---

[2] John Edward Sowerby (1825–1870) was a British botanical illustrator and publisher. Here, the reference is likely to his 1858-60 book *British Wild Flowers*.

ch. ends p. 123

the Man, and the scented orchid and a little later the pyramid orchid and the bee.[3] We try to have as many different kinds as we can in the bowl together all the summer through."

"Do you ever get the fly?"[4]

"Oh, yes, sometimes," said Anwrel.

"Ah, I heard that they grew with you," said the Bishop.

"And sometimes," said Anwrel, getting interested, "we get the Butterfly. There's a wood near Wolding . . ."

"Better not say a word about that," said the Bishop, "not even to me. It's wonderful how such information spreads, and if it got to London you'd have twenty people coming down one Saturday to dig it up, or at any rate tear its roots out."

"That is quite true, my lord," said Anwrel warmly, for he loved to talk with men that understood flowers. But the Bishop left that subject.

"And in the Autumn and Winter?" he asked. "Are you able to find plenty of interests through those months too?"

"I collect worked flints," he said.

"Ah," said the Bishop; "well, you couldn't live in a better place for it. Wolding has, I believe, a name amongst the geologists. It's on the hills that you find them I suppose?"

"Yes, my lord. Especially the eoliths."

"Ah. Yes. Well, they provide very interesting discussions. You know some of them maintain that they have not been worked by man at all?"

"So I believe, my lord."

"And you of course are satisfied that they have been."

"Well I think so. You see I have some that seem to be quite obvious. And if some, why not all? Allowing of course for a percentage of mistakes. They all come from the same level."

And in a moment they would have been debating the whole question of Man's earliest weapons and tools. But from this also the Bishop waved Anwrel away.

---

[3] Yes, he just named seven different types of orchids in a row.

[4] One of several orchids that mimic insects to attract pollinators.

"And what do you find to do in the long evenings?"

"Well, on Saturdays," said Anwrel —

"No, your leisure I mean."

"Well, I play chess sometimes, my lord. The doctor is a good player, and often looks in of an evening during the Winter."

"An excellent game," said the Bishop. "An excellent game. It is not a game, it's a science. A science that never did any man any harm yet. I recommend it to you. Are there others that you can play with besides the doctor?"

"There's the curate at Hooton,"[5] said Anwrel.

"Excellent," answered the Bishop. "And what opening do you play?"

"Usually the Ruy Lopez,"[6] said Anwrel.

"No doubt the best," said the Bishop, "no doubt the best; and yet to get the most out of chess I know nothing, if Black will play it, to equal the Muzio.[7] Really I recommend it to you whenever you have the move. I know that it has been held that, if Black play correctly, White's sacrifice of the knight cannot be justified; but he must play correctly for twenty or thirty moves, and when will you meet so much absolute correctness in chess? No, I play the Muzio whenever I can, and I shall only give it up when I find a player whose correctness can stultify[8] the terrific attack. It is a pearl among openings."

"I will play it, my lord. I certainly will," said Anwrel.

"That's right," said the Bishop, "and I'm sure you'll enjoy it. Well, as you know, a Bishop's time belongs to many people. I'm always in debt for several hours. My chaplain keeps my

---

[5] A suburban village and former civil parish on the Wirral Peninsula, within the ceremonial county of Cheshire, England.

[6] Also called the Spanish Opening, named after Ruy López de Segura, a 16th-century Spanish priest who, in 1561, published the 150-page chess book, *Libro de la invencion liberal y arte del juego del axedrez* ("Book of the liberal invention and art of the game of chess").

[7] A sharp and aggressive chess opening, the Muzio Gambit is a variation of the King's Gambit.

[8] In this context, lessen the enthusiasm for.

ch. ends p. 123

appointments in a book. I call it my overdraft on time. So I'm afraid . . ."

"My lord," exclaimed Anwrel, "before I go. There is one matter of gravest importance to me. I have just come from the cathedral."

"Yes?" said the Bishop encouragingly.

"It is about the gargoyles, my lord. It is one in particular, looking to the South-East."

The Bishop's smile died out. Some grave thought crossed his face, and a moment later he spoke again with all his persuasive authority.

"I shouldn't bother about that," he said.

"No, my lord?" said poor Anwrel.

The Bishop shook his head. "And now . . ."

Good Heavens! The interview was over. And he had got nothing but sanity, sanity, sanity, from three separate men. He was all alone with a problem that demanded the most stupendous effort of brains greater than his, if a doom was to be averted from a whole parish, and the greater the brain the more he got the tact and the sanity that was suited to wonted events and common difficulties. He was sick of sanity. And as he rose to go and saw far down the street out of the large palace window, he saw by an astounding coincidence, as it seemed to him, a man in a very curious assortment of clothes and a most remarkable hat walking that way with the aid of a queer stick, away from the cathedral.

"Might I ask your lordship who that man is?" said Anwrel pointing away.

The Bishop came nearer the window. "Oh, he," he said. "I'm afraid he's not quite right. Harmless, but not all there. He's named Perkin. He's lived here all his life."

"Well I must not detain your lordship," said Anwrel hurriedly, and got out to the street in time to meet that curious man.

So eager was Anwrel for a change from quiet tact, so useless to him in his desperate situation, that he went straight up to the wanderer in the remarkable hat and cheerily said to him, "Well?"

"Hullo," said the wanderer in as friendly a tone. And there they were like two old friends.

"Everything all right?" asked Anwrel.

"Ha, ha," laughed the wanderer. "No."

"It's the same with me," said Anwrel.

"Is it?" said the wanderer quickly. "Take care they don't get after you."

"Who?" asked Anwrel.

"The things that are after me," the old man answered.

"What's the trouble?" asked Anwrel.

"Hist,"[9] said the other, and looked swiftly about him. "I'll tell you"; and, looking once more to see that no one should hear him, "I lost my illusions."

"Lost your illusions?" said Anwrel.

"Yes."

"How did that happen?"

"I'll tell you. I saw the mayor in all his robes one day. I just laughed at it all. I saw tall silk hats and laughed again: I do to this day. And I saw the cathedral with its coloured windows, and I laughed at that too. The illusion went out of everything. That's how it happened."

"I see," said Anwrel. "An agnostic, and probably a socialist, and I'm sorry to hear it. But that doesn't make you mad. They do think you're mad, don't they? You won't mind my saying this? Because I believe they think me a bit mad too."

"No," said the old man, "that doesn't make you mad. Not at once, it doesn't. But when the illusions are gone; oh, man, that's the time to beware. It's the things that pour in on you then. They are what do it."

"Are you much troubled?" asked Anwrel.

"Yes," said the man. "You see my illusions are gone. They're the only defence we have. And the woods of the night are full

---

[9] An archaic exclamation used to attract attention or call for silence.

ch. ends next p.

of all manner of things. When our illusions are down they all pour in."

"Tell me," said Anwrel. "Does Pan ever trouble you?"

"Oh, yes," said the old man. "Him and hundreds more. The woods of the night are full of them."

"And they come and trouble you," said Anwrel.

"Trouble me!" said the old man. "Aye. I've no defence against them. Keep your illusions, man; keep your illusions. Why, many a time I can't sleep all night long for thinking of the futility of the planets going round and round as uselessly as ours through the empty bleakness of Space. And hist! When you are in that mood they get to hear of it, and they come prowling and nosing through the woods of the night. And they get you, they get you when you've nothing to keep them out, if they have to come from the far side of Neptune to do it."

"Neptune," said Anwrel. "You know something of astronomy then."

"Oh, yes," said the old man. "I know lots of things. That's the trouble. I knew too much. And so one day all my illusions went."

"Couldn't you," said Anwrel wistfully and gently, "couldn't you get them back?"

"Not now," said the old man. "The woods of the night have sprouted up all over them."

A policeman was coming across the street to them, for that old man was not allowed to stand still for long, because he was so curious that, whenever he did, a crowd began to collect and would hinder the traffic.

"Walk a little way with me," said Anwrel drawing him from the direction of the policeman. "We have a lot in common, and I should like a talk with you. You see one of these things that troubles you troubles me. I have my illusions yet, but I fear that he is too strong for them. I've asked help of other men, but they give me common sense. Is common sense any good against these things, do you think?"

"Ha, ha, ha," laughed the wanderer. "Ha, ha, ha."

"Not so loud," said Anwrel.

"Ha, ha, ha," the old man went on.

"Then what can help me do you think?" asked Anwrel. "It's Pan that is troubling me."

"There's worse than him in the woods of the night," said the wanderer.

"Then what would you do?" asked Anwrel.

"Why," said the wanderer, "if your illusions are strong enough to keep him out. They'll keep him out all right."

"Yes. Yes, of course," said Anwrel. "But what if they're weaker than he?"

"Why," said the wanderer, "then; why, Pan was always friendly to Man. That's you and me you know. We may have changed a lot this last two thousand years; but that's you and me still. Why, I'd let him come nosing in."

"Not while I can fight him," said Anwrel.

"No," said the wanderer. "Well, I'll walk out soon and see how you're getting on."

"But I live out at Wolding," said Anwrel.

"Well, I'll walk over," the old man said. "It will only take me a week, and I happen to be disengaged this year. And remember, there are worse than Pan in the woods of the night. Goodbye."

And he waved his arm like a plenipotentiary[10] bidding farewell to a fleet.

---

[10] A diplomatic agent fully authorized to represent their government.

24
The Defection of St. Ethelbruda

At that the old man strode away. Anwrel followed at first, for he would have said more to him; but the wanderer went with such strides up a side street, the huge stick seeming to take a part in the striding, the left arm swinging wide and the frock coat flapping hugely, that Anwrel saw after a few steps that he could not keep up with that terrific gait. When he realised that, his hurried pace slowed down to purposeless drifting, and the drift carried him back toward the cathedral without any motive at all. Suddenly he realised that the 5:10 train must have gone. It mattered very little to him: he had no good news to bring back to Wolding: he had left a bag at the station, and would return next day. Again he was under the cathedral walls, looking up at the monstrous flock of grinning shapes that had passed at one time or another across the imagination of man. "Poor fellow," he thought, "They're all after old Perkin." And then he reflected that here was the man to help him, the man through whose mind all these things rioted. The Bishop had the brains for it; but what was the good of that when those brains were resolutely closed to any considerations of such things whatever? And Hetley had the learning for it. But Hetley had heard nothing, and never would hear anything that was not shouted in his ear. Perkin, whatever his brains, had his attention fixed on probably every move of all those things that the Bishop, his chaplain, and Hetley all kept so carefully outside their knowledge. Yes, Perkin was the man. He must see him again.

Thus seeking help in his loneliness had Anwrel come at last to such strange companionship.

He fetched his bag from the station and, shunning the modern inconveniences of the Crozier, returned with it to the Green Man. And there the landlady welcomed him kindly, and looked after him herself; for he somehow seemed to her even more in need of being helped and looked after than he had when she saw him at lunch. A woman that seemed scarcely to have left the thirties behind her, even if she were more than halfway through the next decade; and entering this story with her few moments of kindness, and passing utterly out of it, like a shaft of sunlight briefly pouring its gold through a narrow window upon its way far hence.

"Nice weather," she said as he sat at his supper, and she came to see that he had all that he wanted.

"Yes, indeed," said Anwrel.

"Very nice for the hay."

For a rural parish, of course, was written all over Anwrel; and she supposed his thoughts would be full of the hay just now. Yet what a pang she caused him. Duffin was not cutting his hay yet! A neglect unparalleled in his knowledge of Wolding. Were others delaying too? Would the hay ever be cut that year in Wolding at all?

"Yes," he said.

And she saw that her remark had not been the right one, and was casting round for something more suitable. But he spoke again first.

"I met a very interesting man in the street. I think he was called Perkin. I wonder if you know anything about him."

It was all he could talk of, for he had come desperately to

ch. ends p. 128

Snichester to find help, and Perkin seemed the only man from whom he could ever have it. But she was looking as though the name conveyed nothing whatever to her.

"He has rather a peculiar hat," he added.

"Oh, mad Perkin," she said. "We all know him. He lives here. Sometimes in the workhouse, sometimes he'll lodge at a cottage. He's quite crazy."

"Yes. Yes," muttered Anwrel. "Mr. Hetley. You know him? He comes into Snichester often I suppose?"

"Oh, yes. A very clever gentleman, very clever indeed."

"Yes," said Anwrel. "I suppose he is. They say the Bishop is very clever too."

"Oh, yes," she answered. "They say he's the cleverest we've had here for many a year."

Well, it was clear what side she was on. And, kind though she seemed, it was clear he would get no help from her, this man so urgently in need of help. It is terrible when from kindness itself, help cannot even be looked for. One is in a sore strait then. From Perkin alone could it come: there was the will to help him, and there the knowledge. Toward such he was being driven.

He talked for a while with her of hay, of the cathedral, of the supply of tourists, of anything but what was in his mind. Then he said goodnight, and sat and smoked for a while, and thought prodigiously and to little purpose.

In the bright morning he said farewell to the landlady of the Green Man, and walked with his bag to the station, and left Snichester.

So struck was he by the old wanderer's advice, for he leaned heavily now on any help he could get, that he sent no wire to Spelkins, as he had arranged, to tell him the train he would come by, but hired a fly at Seldham and drove part of the way to Wolding, stopping at the back of the downs, a not expensive journey: thence he could walk again to Ethelbruda's tomb, and down the hill home. For it seemed to him wise to strengthen his illusions; and where better than at that miracle-working tomb, where lay, as tradition told, that enemy of the pagans, famed throughout all the diocese? Not miracle-working quite, perhaps; for its wonders were too small to be named miracles; but no one doubted in Wolding that, if you rubbed a wart on a certain part of the tomb that was always moist with old rain, the wart would go away in two or three days. So, leaving his bag at Seldham for the carter[1] that drove to Wolding on Wednesdays and Saturdays, he drove to the foot of the downs, and there went up from the road, by a slope that could just be climbed without using one's hands. When he got to the top he came to level fields, dipping every here and there into little valleys, that earlier in the year were marvellous places for primroses[2] wherever they had the shelter of hedges or shaws. Across these fields he strolled, his thoughts full of the words of the crazed old wanderer of Snichester. And presently there was the tomb rising up before him, above a clump of brambles out in a field.

And there he had intended to meditate long, until strong hopes and spiritual fortitudes should come to him in answer to his great need. He did not feel that Death had entirely annihilated, even here on earth, that mighty champion of the downland's Christianity, for she worked for them still although with but humble wonders.

He had barely seen the tomb when he noticed coming toward him a man who lived on the lonely edge of his parish in the unfrequented country far from Wolding, a small farmer with gnarled hands that had to do most of the work that his farm required.

"Good morning, sir," said the farmer.

"Good morning, Welkin," the vicar replied, not stopping, for he wanted to be alone.

"She no longer cures warts, sir," said Welkin.

"What!" cried the vicar, almost with a tone of anguish.

---

[1] Someone whose work is driving carts, or open two-wheeled carriages.

[2] A commonly cultivated plant that produces showy five-lobed pale yellow flowers in the early spring.

ch. ends next p.

"She doesn't cure warts any more."

Was it one of the illusions falling down already? He had come for help, and the champion was weaker at the very moment of his greatest need of her strength. All, all were failing him.

"Oh, but are you sure?" he asked.

"Came here last Friday, sir, and again on Saturday. Should be beginning to take effect by now."

Friday and Saturday; the very days that so much had been happening in Wolding.

"Try again, Welkin, try again," said the vicar.

"Just been trying, sir, but it won't be any good."

Welkin went on and left the vicar lonelier yet. Why! There was no limit to the help that he might have rightly demanded, to meet this terrible crisis. And everywhere they failed him. And here was Ethelbruda quietly falling asleep. Piqued, perhaps. And rightly, too. And yet how weak, how feeble, to turn to womanish pique at such a moment, when she should have risen in armour!

These were the thoughts of the vicar: they were not just; but he was driven to them by his continual rebuffs from all that should have helped him.

25. The Defection of Mrs. End

It was late for lunch when the vicar came home, but Augusta had seen him coming down the hill and had waited till he got in. And almost the first question he asked was "Where are the letters?" For he had just missed the morning post the day before, though he had thought that it should have been in before he started; and now there should be that post and the evening post, as well as one this morning. He had been looking forward to this; for he set store by the change that the post would bring to any mood, with the news and the views of others, that might be at any distance from the cares that were vexing him. Not often did a post fulfil his expectations, and then one day a letter would come that would entirely absorb him for half an hour, perhaps for the whole morning. Upon what subject? Some trifle. It is not any intrinsic matter that there is in things themselves, on which their value depends to us, but it is on their power to awaken in us enthusiasm.

A postcard comes for instance addressed to some elderly gentleman living alone, and nothing is on it but **36 . . . Q×KBP+**.[1]

---

[1] Re: Chess — 36th move, Queen captures King's Bishop Pawn, check.

"From some foreign gentleman," says the post-mistress. And her thoughts rise far from the fields in which folk speak English, and are awhile in strange lands with monkeys and coconuts, Russians and French and Italians, glimpsing things she will never see, abroad and afar where her lot will never take her; dreaming inaccurate nonsense, some might say; yet when she comes back in two moments to the counter of the dingy little post office she is the better for that short holiday of the spirit. "Arithmetic," says the postman on his rounds, seeing the plus sign and the multiplication sign and the numbers. A drab thing to him. And if it takes him back for a moment to his youth, and the bright companions he had, it takes him back to a shadow that fell over him and them. It was all right at first when one added figures to figures, and the Spring mornings were brighter then than now; but when it came to adding and multiplying letters of the alphabet, that was a bit too much. No, the postcard fails to awaken any winged interest here. But when it comes to the villa, and the maid takes it. A single glance, and she knows. "Nihilists," she says! A bright "Good morning," to the postman, and her heart full of mystery and bombs. As blackguardly[2] a code as was ever put together. And that quiet old gentleman: so he was in with *them!* The creaky boards of the villa creak now with a delightfully sinister meaning, and dingy corners now hide dreadful secrets. What will come of it all? Only the cook will know that. So the postcard is delivered with a wonderful outward calm, and away she goes to the kitchen. And the lonely old gentleman with his postcard, a change comes over him. Powers that that villa and all the neighbouring village have no use for muster and march to his mind. He has a name far from here, and amongst a few. And he sees that his strength is not deserting him. Of the hard-earned admiration that they accord him he sees he is worthy yet. "Wasting time that he can't afford, in capturing pawns," he mutters over his postcard. Then to his chessboard, and the room is silent.

---

[2] Unscrupulous or unprincipled.

So Elderick Anwrel, hoping for the change that a letter would sometimes bring to tired thoughts, asked for the post.

"The postman didn't come today," said Augusta.

"Didn't he?" said the vicar. "But where's yesterday's post?"

"He didn't come yesterday either," she said with a tired voice.

"What. No letters for anyone?" he said. "Spelkins, or Mrs. Tweedy? And none for you, by either post?"

"He didn't bring any," she said.

There were relations outside this story who should have written, and interests scarce worthy of chronicling that might have brought him a letter.

"That is strange," he said.

But she made no comment.

They entered the dining-room. And there on the sideboard stood their silver teapot, that used at breakfast-time to add so much to the brightness of the morning, just catching the sunlight and throwing it dazzlingly back. They thought a good deal of that teapot. But now it stood there as dull as any part of the corner in which the sideboard was.

"The teapot hasn't been cleaned," said Anwrel with some surprise.

"No," said Augusta.

"What can Marion have been thinking of?" he said.

Would he not see that things were all different now?

She made no answer: she was waiting to hear if he had got help in Snichester. She could think of nothing else. A strained silence passed while she waited. But as soon as he was seated at the table and still had not spoken, she said to him: "Well? You saw Hetley?"

"Yes. Oh, yes," he said.

"You'll get help?" she asked.

"Well, no, not from him," he replied.

"He won't help us?" she gasped.

"Well, no," he said. "You see he didn't hear anything."

"He didn't hear anything," she said.

"No. Not when he was here."

ch. ends p. 136

"But he must have," she said. "Tommy Duffin was playing the pipes every evening while we were away. He must have heard them."

"I'm afraid not," he said.

"Why! He must be deaf," she said.

"I'm afraid so," said Anwrel.

There was a long silence as though a blow had fallen on her. And she looked worn already. Then she found a hope with difficulty, and spoke again.

"You said you didn't get help from him. But you got help?" she asked.

"Well, yes," he said.

"From the Bishop?" she asked.

"Well, no," said Anwrel.

"The chaplain?"

"No. No, I don't think he'd help us."

"We must have help," came from her bitterly as a cry.

"Yes, indeed," he said.

"Who'll help us?" she asked.

"Well, there's a man," he answered, "who . . . Of course one can't judge people by their dress."

"No," she said, puzzled.

"Nor by their reputation," he went on: "the world's judgment is not accurate enough for that. Nor by their appearance, for that's setting our own judgment up too high. No, I trusted to the Bishop, and he sent us Hetley. I spoke to the chaplain and Hetley too. It's the same everywhere. The thing's too fantastic for them and we must look elsewhere."

"But where?" she said.

"The man I told you of."

"But what man?" she asked.

"A man I met in Snichester."

"What's he like?"

"It's not by appearances we can judge him."

"What kind of man is he?" she said.

"He's one," he replied, "who has seen all these things."

"What things?" she asked.

"The things that are troubling us."

"You mean . . . ?"

"Yes," he said. "The Reverend Arthur Davidson, if he pleases to call himself that. I met a man who has seen such."

"But . . ." she gasped.

"There is no one else," he said, "that can help us now."

And then she wanted to know who he was and exactly how he would help them.

"He is named Perkin," he said. "And he will come and give me advice as to how to deal with it."

"When will he come?" she asked.

"Oh, in a week or so," he said.

"A week!" she exclaimed. "We must have help at once."

And the look of strain on her face increased, as though it were all a matter of hours.

"At once?" he said. "He can't come at once. There is no really urgent hurry."

"Can't you see," she said, "that they'll all go over the hill? They'll all go to the Old Stones and leave you!"

She glanced round as though at any moment the call to go might be sounded.

"They still come to church," he said.

"Only because Tommy Duffin lets them," she answered. "If he were to blow those pipes outside the church door . . ."

"The Bishop would have to take action then," he said.

"It would be too late, then," she said. "Too late."

And she spoke with an impatience that sounded new to Anwrel.

"Mrs. Duffin must know all about it by now," he said. "Perhaps she may knock it all out of him yet."

"Go and see her," she replied strangely.

What had made this change in Augusta? What could be happening?

"What are they doing now," he asked, "down in the village?"

ch. ends p. 136

"Go and look," she said, and said no more than that. And the strained look came back to her face as she sat silent.

"Very well. I will," said Anwrel.

The vicar went down to the village pondering wearily as usual. He was wondering when help would come, and whether that strange man who had promised help, and had known the things that haunt the shadowy spaces of legend and guess, just out beyond the borders of human knowledge, would be able to save Wolding. He should be able to, for he had seen what most men could not see and others would not: he alone would not be fighting in the dark if he bore arms against Pan. But then again the enemy was so ancient: and it hardly seemed that an upstart visionary like Perkin, however much he had seen and known, could overthrow him now.

So ran the swift troubled thoughts, which ever since the vicar first wrote to the Bishop had been always seeking help. Perhaps there had been a time when Anwrel would have relied more on himself, but now he needed help as a man in the grip of a torrent, and swept under, needs air. Full of his meditations, a dull figure to look on, yet alert with swift thoughts within, he nearly ran into old Hibbuts coming up the hill; Hibbuts the sexton,[3] and secretary of the Horticultural Society, who year in year out had always come up to him at the Vicarage on the same date and with the same words, which began "About this Flower Show, sir . . . " And then they would go together over tiny absorbing details, during which the big hand of the clock would move round unnoticed, as though Time had seized this opportunity to steal an hour from Man: and next day the Wolding Flower Show would be announced. And that date was three days ago, last Saturday. And Hibbuts had never come. The vicar suddenly remembered it.

"Hullo Hibbuts," he said.

"Good morning, sir," said Hibbuts.

---

[3] One who looks after a church and churchyard.

"You never came about the Flower Show, Hibbuts."

"Didn't I, sir?" said Hibbuts.

"No," said the vicar. "We should have had the notices out by now."

"So we should, sir."

"But you never came," said Anwrel.

"I must have forgotten it, sir," said Hibbuts.

"I've never known you forget it before," said the vicar. "Well, we'd better go over it this evening."

"Why, yes, sir," said Hibbuts. "We must have the Flower Show the same as ever."

"Of course," said the vicar.

"We must have something of the sort, sir; even if . . . "

"Even if what?"

"Oh, nothing, sir," said Hibbuts.

"Then you will come up after tea?"

"Oh, I don't mind if I do, sir," said Hibbuts.

The vicar looked at him, finding his answer strange. And, whether the man had secrets to hide from that steady gaze, or whether he resented the searching rays of it, he suddenly said to the vicar, "I don't think there'll be no Flower Show this year, sir."

"No Flower Show? But there must be," said the vicar.

"Yes, sir?" said Hibbuts.

"Why not?" said the vicar.

"Oh, I don't know, sir," said the sexton.

"Why not?" Anwrel asked again.

"I really couldn't say, sir. I must be going on now."

And Hibbuts went, and though the vicar called after him "Why?" he knew well enough: the old ways of Wolding were beginning to fall before customs older and stronger.

The vicar walked on, still uselessly pondering, and came to a field by the road, in which was a wealth of hay, starred by dog-daisies. He gazed out over it till he saw in a corner one

ch. ends next p.

man mowing a bit of it with a scythe.[4] It was too far to hail him. But there was the fact; one man with a scythe in a field of thirty acres that should have all been cut already. There was no difficulty in obtaining a cutter: not every farmer had one of those machines, but Drover up on the hill always had one for hire, and there were plenty more.

The vicar walked on. And now he came to the first house in the village, a cottage whose white doorstep he knew as well as astronomers know some large star. The steps had not been whitewashed. And next he came to some children, at play in the street. But it was school-time! He went up to them and they rather moved away from him, as rooks[5] move away from a man that is riding a horse, not scattering, as from one who walks, yet edging away. But he came up to one of them, a girl of eleven, feeling with all his heart as he came that he was a hostile figure to them. She faced him, with the sun on her bright locks, and a look of impudent courage, standing alone.

"Why are you not in school, Nancy?" he said.

"Mrs. End isn't taking school this afternoon," she said.

"Why not?" said the vicar.

"I don't know. She isn't here."

"What did you learn this morning?" he asked, on the track of the truth of the matter.

"It was to have been arithmetic," said Nancy.

"Was to have been," said the vicar. "But what did you learn?"

"Mrs. End said it wouldn't matter."

"Wouldn't matter! Why?"

"She said, Mrs. End did," said Nancy, "that we shouldn't want arithmetic any more."

---

[4] A manual tool with a long handle and a long, curved single-edged blade that moves in a plane parallel to the ground, used for mowing, cutting, or reaping by hand. Often depicted being wielded by Death or the Grim Reaper.

[5] Eurasian crows.

26

The Fire on the Stone

So the vicar went on to the post office and took a telegraph form, and addressed it to Perkin, Snichester, and signed it The Vicar of Wolding, and added the one word Come.

Listlessly Mrs. Datchery, the post-mistress, pushed a bundle of letters toward him that had been lying there all day, the letters for the Vicarage. The vicar took them and left.

He might have seen much more of the change that had come over the village, but he had seen enough; here the work of a day neglected in a garden, there the work of the year some while overdue in a hayfield; a listlessness everywhere; a rose, once trained to a wall, broken loose, and left to wave with the wind; a man's tie all ill-tied and flapping loose over his coat; gates that should be shut left open; and everywhere an air of dreamy preoccupation with something far from those fields, and far indeed from the quiet orderly ways that Wolding had known through Elderick Anwrel's time, and far before that as long as there was any memory. One strange experience Wolding had had, and the fruits of it ripened now, filling Anwrel's spirit with bitterness. He had seen enough, and he went back through the village, and felt as he walked there by the doors of his own parishioners, almost as the inhabitant of a conquered country might feel, walking in cities occupied by the victors; almost, but not quite yet, for he rested his hope on Perkin, to whom these terrible wonders were not strange.

Now he returned to the vicarage to wait for Hibbuts, whom he had told to come up after tea.

"Well?" said Augusta.

"Yes, it's all changed," he said. "All changed."

"What will you do?" she asked anxiously.

"I've sent for Perkin," he said. "The man I told you of."

"Will he be able to stop it?" she said.

"I told you," he said. And then more patiently and slowly he went on: "It's like this, Augusta: this thing that is happening isn't like ordinary things. It doesn't happen in other parishes. It isn't in modern books. It should have all died out thousands of years ago. I wish to Heaven it had! But it isn't in modern thought at all. And it isn't studied now; so able scholars can't help me."

"The Bishop should have helped us for all that," sighed Augusta.

"No," said Anwrel. "It was impossible. It's outside modern thought. He feared that I might be mad, and he examined me to see. And even now I think he isn't sure. If I asked him for help again he would have no doubt of it."

"Then I don't see how Perkin can help," she said.

"Can't you see?" he said. "Can't you see? Perkin has known these things. He's the very man that *can* help."

"Know them?" she said. "How can he know them?"

"He sees them all round him," said the vicar.

"But. But is he mad?" she said.

"Oh, can't you see," said poor Anwrel, "that sanity cannot save us?"

She thought a long while over that. "No," she said, "no. It never will."

They kept silence then, such a silence as beleaguered troops might keep, sitting down to eat rats. They seemed nearing their last extremity.

And then she asked: "When will he come?"

"He said a week," he answered.

Then they sat silent again.

"I told Hibbuts to come up after tea," he said at last. "We are going to talk over the Flower Show."

"He'll never come," she said.

And they had tea, and they waited; but Augusta was right and Hibbuts never came. And instead of Hibbuts came that awful messenger, the music that had strayed from Arcadian slopes and down the long ages, to float over fields of England from Tommy Duffin's pipes. It came with its clear message to them both, to leave that house and all that the vicarage stood for, and all that the last two thousand years had taught, and to turn again and remember the Old Stones. And what was there to know of the Old Stones? "Come and I'll tell you. Come and I'll tell you. Come and I'll tell you," sang the strange tune like chimes.

Augusta gripped both arms of her chair, and her face went tense and white. The vicar watched her reproachfully. "You too?" he said gravely when the music stopped.

"I didn't go," she almost screamed.

"Go, indeed!" said the vicar. "No, of course not."

The idea of Augusta going had never entered his mind; though the thought of going himself had come, however manfully he cast it out; had come often.

She did not answer and Anwrel said no more. So they sat silent.

Again she asked him when Perkin would come, and again he told her a week.

"But when he gets your wire," she urged.

"He will walk," he said. "He'll start today and should be here on Monday."

"But why can't he come by train?" she asked.

It was hard for him to explain. Man has imagined many

ch. ends p. 142

things: some of them he has put forth in iron and steel, and others have remained within his imagination. Both kinds are equally wonderful; but the things of iron and steel attract the more attention because they parade continually before our eyes and our ears, and indeed all our five senses, and the mind is always having reports of them from these alert five; while the things that have remained within the imagination, and that, but for an occasional statue or work on bronze, have never been clothed with matter, lurk in the vastnesses of the skull with all that man has known, and are only seen now and then by the inner eye amongst the lumber of ages. It was with these things that Perkin was concerned, not with the other wonders, nor did Anwrel wish that his ally's restless thoughts should be turned from the matter in hand to consider the mystery of such things as trains.

But it was hard to explain all this to one who had never seen Perkin, though once you had seen him and talked with him it was obvious. So he merely said, "Oh, Perkin would never come by train."

And this she accepted.

The influence of the pipes had gone far and deep. Here was the vicarage gloomy and silent because of them, that only a while ago was a cheery little house.

A week of waiting before any help would come. And that look on Augusta's face. The vicar rose and went to his study and began to turn over his collection of flint implements, every one numbered on a little square piece of sticking-paper, and a notebook with date and place against every number, recalling old journeys over high brown fields of clay above the hills of chalk. But they brought him no solace today. They did not lure his thoughts from the ruin of Wolding, nor calmed his fears busy with guesses of how the end would be. Only the old blue palaeolith seemed glancing toward him, sideways out of its hollows, with a crudely familiar look, as though he were coming nearer and nearer to this blunt primitive thing, across a gap in the ages. About supper time the vicar rose from his flints and went away from the house. He was not hungry; and a troubled mind drove him out to walk swiftly, as though with plodding feet there came some scrap of harmony between body and brain, that would not come to him sitting still in a chair while his thoughts raced on and on. And the theme of his thoughts was the same old theme that comes to all minds in trouble, a balance, always shifting, between the evil as one fears it and the help as one hopes it. How bad were things with the village? How soon would Perkin come? Nothing else occupied his mind all the evening.

I will not chronicle such mournful thoughts. Let us follow instead the body, the dark coat and the felt hat, that they drove onward. We do not always see the spirit clearly outlined in that shadow that it casts on earth, and that has chief honours here, the human body; but it was clear enough in the appearance of Anwrel, a woebegone[1] figure. One of the conquered indeed; for in every neglected thing he passed, as he strode swiftly again through the village, he saw something that, if it were only a neatness about a garden or a tidiness about a path, was a part of the olden ways now overthrown, and a new joy had come to the village, a joy in which he could take no part while anathema[2] had any meaning to him. He saw young men with circles of roses on their bare heads: he passed them hurriedly. And as he climbed Wold Hill beyond the village he saw, running over the slope toward Mrs. Airland's, Lily wearing a wreath of convolvulus[3] in her hair. Then he knew that he should find them gone from the Old Stones, and he pressed on to find what traces he could see of this new worship; how far they had got; well knowing that, when the ceremonial of it became more intricate or in any way ampler than that of the lawful and right service he held, it would be the end of his ministrations. What they did at the Old Stones he knew not, not even knowing of

---

[1] Sad or miserable.

[2] A curse or denunciation pronounced by ecclesiastical authority.

[3] A twining plant of the morning glory family with bright trumpet-shaped flowers and triangular leaves, sometimes referred to as bindweed.

ch. ends next p.

their ritual dance: one thing he dreaded more than everything else, barely letting his thoughts hint it; he dreaded lest they should make sacrifice there, offering burnt offerings unto heathen gods. After that, if it came to that, after that they would never come to his church again.

When the vicar came to the beeches amongst which gnarled yew-trees stood, that had known the hill before ever the beech-trees came, night seemed to enter the wood with him. For some while now the Evening Star had been seen, but the sky was still full of daylight; and, like a pale sapphire in a setting of diamonds, the planet was shining through that other light. To the hushed wood the daylight came no longer, and the flash of the Evening Star above the branches was the only clear light that the vicar saw, as he went uphill over the twisted roots. At the top he rested, sitting down on a root, alone with those ceaseless thoughts. And for some while he stayed there, for it was a steep climb up from the village, though the last part of it was of necessity slow because of the dark of the wood. Then he rose and went down the far slope past beech and pine, going softly without a sound, a spy in his own parish. And so he came to the edge of the wood and looked out on the other valley, standing behind a tree and peering carefully round it at the Old Stones of Wolding clustered below in their field. No one was there, but there was a glow on the stones.

He walked toward them and saw the sides turned inward, those that were furthest from him, glowing like ruddy faces. And soon he saw the soft dance of wavering shadows, that had not danced perhaps for ages and ages, flickering up and down whenever a breeze would dance with them. And there on the long flat stone was a flame as light as a fairy, lucidly burning in the midst of the circle with the steady light that comes from spirit or oil, with which someone had soaked some rags, and had left them to burn all night. And an awful memory of something Hetley had said of a cave near the Acropolis struck the vicar as sudden and chill as the wind that blows before thunder.

27

Mrs. Duffin Takes Sunday School

Those were anxious days for the vicar, and yet he did nothing useful. He investigated and watched. He saw the village drifting all that week, like a derelict galleon,[1] with cable rusted through, that a current takes away out of a harbour, slowly to cold grey distance. And, as lights and landmarks would vanish one by one from the sight of any mariner lost with the galleon, some derelict of the race of men, doomed to the derelict ship; so many a custom, many an ancient way, many remembered trifles, that were always the first to welcome the homing thoughts of absent Wolding men, faded away that week and were lost in the wastes of Time. It especially pained the vicar, although he could not say why, that Blegg was no longer clipping the yew in his garden to keep it shaped like a peacock. In another garden the hollyhocks drooped and broke, through not being properly tied. And nowhere was the hay being properly cut. And the heathen rites continued. All this the vicar watched, a melancholy figure haunting the evening, but still he did nothing himself.

[1] A large three-masted sailing ship used especially by Spain as merchant ships or warships from the 15th to the 18th centuries.

Had physical action been demanded he would have taken his part, at his age, and even against a hundred men. For everywhere the physical is limited. But this was spiritual and he looked for help, had looked for it ever since this story began, and was waiting for it yet. The telegram had undoubtedly been sent; it was one of the last that anyone had troubled to send from Wolding; and no message had come to say it had not been delivered. So he knew that the brief address had been sufficient to find that curious figure. There seemed nothing to do but to wait.

Sometimes he thought that Augusta, by some silence, implied that he ought to act himself. But how? No one less than a bishop, he felt, could advise him in such a spiritual crisis. Or Perkin. A man perpetually tossed on spiritual storms. A mariner of the unknown.

So he waited, and prayed for Perkin. Once in that week he forlornly climbed the hill on his side of the valley, and went over the downs to see Welkin. He found him in a field.

"Well," he said, "Welkin; those warts getting any better?"

"No, sir. She can't cure 'em."

It was as the vicar had feared.

"She's lost the knack of it, sir," Welkin went on.

"She could do it," broke out the vicar, "only she won't."

"It's my belief, sir," said Welkin, "as she can't."

"She could do it," the vicar repeated bitterly. "She could do it." And he went away mumbling the same words to himself, and brooding on the failure of help wherever it was most due.

Once in these days he met Tommy Duffin, out on the hill in the morning, and stopped and spoke with him, and realised from the unintelligent face that here was no young genius leading people away from ways that were wearing out to things that were new; but that the body and brain of Tommy Duffin were but the halting-place of some strayed power, that was moving out of the past on a journey none knew whither.

"Going to play those pipes again this evening, Tommy?" he asked directly.

"I don't know, sir," said Tommy.

"What, you're not going to play them this evening?"

"Oh, I don't know, sir."

Yes that was it. A strayed power. And Tommy no more than a mossy stone in a stream, on which a traveller rests his foot for a moment. How should the moss know why?

And all that week the little eternal things were coming softly back; bindweed was climbing up to daylight above the tops of the hedges, weeds visited gardens and stayed unmolested with their more gorgeous kin, tiny plants found homes unreproved in crevices amongst steps, tendrils exploring the air began to lean out across paths; moss heard the news and came quietly to chosen places, unnoticed and almost invisible, but dreaming of long long sojourn and quiet growth that should conquer all but the outlines of all whereon it seized; and ivy heard, and planned or hoped or trusted, for, while each small leaf is caring for nothing but to turn out to the sun, the deep core of the ivy that drives the sap to the tendrils dreams sullenly and alone of the overthrowing of cities. And rabbits came upon little lawns, and grew bolder and found the lettuces; and something taught foxes that they could come further down the slopes; for an awe was departing from man in the village of Wolding, now that he was turning back from the path that steam and steel had shown him, to ways that were more of the Earth that the foxes knew.

All that week the little weeds came straggling back like the soldiers of a scattered army returning after defeat, and rallying on the lost field once again, as indeed they were; for the war with the weeds is won wherever a village is made, though the beaten green army comes back at last in the end.

And all these days, with the village going from bad to worse, the vicar believed that his cause was not lost yet; for he clung to a hope that Mrs. Duffin, a steady church-going woman, would yet reprove her son and put an end to the piping. If that hope failed him, nothing remained but Perkin.

And it came round to Sunday, five days after the wire had gone to Perkin, six days, counting the day on which he must

ch. ends p. 149

have got it; and seven days from Snichester to Wolding made an easy walk, even for an elderly man: it might be done in less.

And they came to church again.

All, then, was by no means lost. The vicar wondered that he could see no trace of gladness in Augusta's face, sitting in a pew before him.

He did not preach any special words to them. There was no need to, for he awaited advice from Perkin as to what line to take; and he had his hopes of Mrs. Duffin, whose bonnet he could clearly see; so that this trouble might all blow over yet. It was her turn to take Sunday School today. If she still did that, and still came to church, things were not so bad with the village as they might look at first sight, whatever Mrs. End did. Sunday School was at three: he would go and see Mrs. Duffin there: he had meant to see her before.

Though he did not preach to them with any especial appeal that should lure them homeward from their perilous straying, yet he read the first two commandments[2] with a gravity such as he seldom used. Indeed, after the first commandment, which he uttered in a voice that was thrillingly clear, he paused for some moments that the words might sink through the silence. And perhaps their effect was felt; but more than this was needed in such a crisis. And when the service was over Augusta said never a word of this. He knew then that she felt that he should make some great effort himself. Well, he would when Perkin came.

Again they met Mr. and Mrs. Duffin coming away from church, though Tommy was not with them.

"You're taking Sunday School today," said the vicar. "Aren't you, Mrs. Duffin?"

"Well, sir," began Mrs. Duffin.

"Yes, you're going. You said so this morning," said Duffin. "Yes, she's going to be there, sir."

"Well, yes, I'm going," said Mrs. Duffin, "but——"

---

[2] I. Thou shalt have no other gods before me.
    II. Thou shalt not make unto thee any graven image.

It was all he wanted to hear. "Oh, that's all right," said the vicar.

Up at the vicarage Anwrel sat down to lunch full of a cheerfulness that for many days had wandered far away from him. Sunday School, after all, more than counterbalanced the defection of Mrs. End. While Sunday School continued and people came to church he still held the parish for the cause that was right and just, whatever enemy might prowl on its borders. With Mrs. Duffin holding out at the Sunday School, and the arrival of his new ally daily expected, things might come right even yet. The vicar's spirits rose, but Augusta sat silent with a look on her face that, if you caught it with a sidelong glance, not staring at it direct, seemed almost a look of dread.

Somehow the time seemed to drag rather heavily; but when it came near three the vicar left the house, and walked down the hill to receive and to give encouragement in the little schoolroom where he pictured the Christian cause holding back for long the forces of paganism. The road was oddly empty. Not a soul did he see till he met with old Mrs. Tichener, coming away from the Sunday School. The old woman saw where he was going.

"I shouldn't go there, sir," she said.

"Go where, Mrs. Tichener?" he asked, not crediting her with having seen his gaze fixed full at the school, nor his deliberate pace, still less with having known the thoughts that were troubling him, or with being able to put two and two together more rapidly than he would even see one of the twos.

"School, sir," said Mrs. Tichener.

"Not go to the school!" said the vicar. "Why not?"

"Oh, I don't know, sir."

"But why not?"

"Oh, it was only a fancy of mine, sir."

Oh, the mystery of these villagers, when you asked them a plain question. Again and again he had noticed it. It was like a wall suddenly erected; no, something more primitive than that; like a hurdle suddenly lifted to keep out a wolf. It was thus that they would bar any further encroachment of an educated mind, if once they began to fear it was coming towards them. She had wished to tell him something, but any sudden enquiry from him, and it was like the wolf coming nearer: up went the barrier, and no questions of his would get him further now. What fancy of hers, what trivial treasure of her mind, would he have hurt if he had been allowed a little nearer to her thoughts? Well, it was no use trying to get further. He would go and see for himself.

And still she stood and watched him and seemed to wish to dissuade him. Tiresome old woman: why couldn't she give her reason? No, their queer old lore was enough for these old women: they never cared about reasons.

"I wouldn't go, sir," she called after him. As he went by a window he saw Mrs. Duffin seated at the desk, and the school-room, as far as he could see, very much fuller than usual. Many of the older lads were there, though children were there too. Mrs. Duffin with her jet brooch and black bonnet, sitting there at the desk, gave him for a moment a confidence in the inviolability[3] of the old order of things, such as a banner suddenly blown might have given to soldiers, rallying in ancient wars. And then a curious sound made him stand still to listen. Mrs. Duffin was chanting. She was chanting words slowly. And the words were not entirely English. "Egg, oh, pan, pan, tone, tone," they went, and a little further. Then she stopped and repeated them. It was thus that the vicar was able to get a part of them accurately— "Egg, oh, pan, pan, tone, tone, lofone, R. K. D." Then the chant went on to words that he could not remember. But there were memories for him in it. Here a word and there a word, and each one calling him back like old chimes to Cambridge. Why! It was Greek. He did not count himself a scholar. But he had not forgotten all his Greek, from the old days at Cambridge. And it was queer how the sound of those words after all these years brought back the Cam to him and the boats; and, oh dear me, youth. But Greek here, in the schoolroom at

---

[3] The state or quality of being unable to be violated, broken, or infringed upon, because it is secure and must be kept sacred or protected.

Wolding! What was she doing. And suddenly the words came to him. The few syllables he could remember at the beginning of the strange chant ran together and formed words, and the words made a fragment of a coherent sentence.

ἐγω παν παντων των λοφων Αρκαδιου βασιλευς.

He did not know what λοφων meant: he looked it up afterward and found that it was slopes. Meanwhile he guessed valleys and was not far out.

"I Pan, of all the Arcadian valleys, King . . ."

So that was what she was teaching them. Something so beautiful and strange and, aye, damnable, that it had lingered on and on for all these years in her memory. And the vicar shouted aloud: "The accursed blessing of Pan!"

28
Arming for the Struggle

When Anwrel returned to the vicarage that afternoon, and Augusta looked up at him from her chair without saying anything, he answered her thoughts with the words:— "Yes, I must do something myself."

When he said that he must do something, it went without saying, considering the enemy that he faced, that it must be the very utmost of which human effort was capable.

Augusta nodded.

"But why, why did he come here?" cried Anwrel.

She looked out at the pleasant slope across the valley, with the sun on the grass, all wild, not harmed at all by anything that had changed the world in the restless 19th century. It got the sun all the morning and all the afternoon, and at evening the shadows came stealing down from the wood. In late summer the thyme would go rioting over the slope like bands of fairy children, and all the golden evening air would be heavy with its wild scent. And all through early summer the briar rose so scented passing breezes that she wondered how far the wandering fragrance went, and whether it came, if only perceived in dreams, to cities where folk knew nothing of briar rose. Not to men perhaps; but certainly to moths, that with their green eyes shining sailed up that stream of fragrance. It was indeed a pleasant slope.

"Why not?" she said. "If he came back at all."

And still his mind was full of all the other places he might have gone to, with his sly pretence of being a clergyman. Why not to one of them instead of Wolding? Such thoughts are common to all troubles.

"There's something about the valley he must have liked," she said.

"Weren't there hundreds of other valleys for him?" he asked bitterly, and unreasonably. For he gave no thought to a factory here, a factory there, and a whole new town in the next place; and villas going up on hillside after hillside, arising out of no feeling in any human mind and reflecting no feeling back, brief monuments to pretentiousness, that would be down in two hundred years; and everywhere machinery with teeth and claws of steel getting its grip on the earth, that had belonged but a while ago to Man and his poor relations. There were not so many valleys, after all, that were unspoiled like this one.

But still he uttered the cry of all minds that first come on a trouble: "Why here?"

"There must be something about it," she said.

"But what?" he asked.

"Don't you remember," she said, "how a wandering goat came to Wold Hill some years ago, and seemed to like it and stayed. It only died there last year. There must be something about the hill."

And still it seemed to him that such a thing, if it happened at all, should have happened to some other parish.

"They said he was dead, you know. They said he was dead. Something like two thousand years ago."

"Did they?" she muttered.

"It wasn't true," he sighed.

But all this was leading them nowhere.

"What will you do?" she said directly.

ch. ends p. 154

"Perkin will come tomorrow," he said.

"And then?" she asked.

"I'll wait for Perkin."

An inner estimate of the enormous effort required of him made him dally a little longer. And he still clung a little to his habit of looking for help. A weakness perhaps. And yet, was he not right to report to the Bishop? Was he not right to consult the greatest scholar in the diocese and to expect sound advice from Hetley? They had failed him, and he waited for Perkin now. And Monday came but not Perkin.

On Tuesday Augusta reminded him gently of his resolution.

"Perkin could only have come yesterday," he said, "if he had started the moment he got my wire. The full week will only be up this evening."

On Wednesday evening she said to him suddenly: "Do you think Perkin will come?"

"Yes," he said, "I am sure of it."

Next day she repeated the question.

"Give him one more day," he said.

On Friday he scarcely spoke all the morning. And in the afternoon he suddenly rose from his chair and said: "I am going to prepare my sermon." And left the drawing-room and went across to his study.

She knew then by his voice, which in that short sentence went all the way from despair to resolution, that he was going to struggle at last, manfully and alone.

Yes it was come to that. All had failed him now. And if his parish was to be saved it must be saved by his own effort. He must preach to them. He must expose in clear unsparing words the error of their heresy. And then he must lead them back to the ways from which they had strayed, by argument as sound as learning could make it and simple enough to harmonise with the thoughts of the simplest of his parishioners. But first it must be sound and logical, and well based upon Holy Writ.

He had his Bible before him and all his books of reference, and his white sheet of foolscap and the red and black ink-pots;

but not a word would come. He sat there for an hour, and still the paper was blank. Still he sat on. It is seldom that a man tries as Anwrel was trying now, and finds that nothing comes as the fruit of such intensity. Yet nothing came to Anwrel. He needed the spirit of Euclid[1] with the research of Macaulay.[2] He needed instances, whether in the Bible itself, or in the writings of the early fathers, or in some modern work of learned ecclesiastics, that should confound this heresy; and then he required to prove, for it was of no use merely quoting, that these great authorities were indubitably right. But no such instance could he find upon which to build his argument. Nothing on which even to begin the long proof that should convince the minds of his people that they had been doing utterly wrong; without which convincing he knew now that they would go so far astray, that when the scandal spread to the ears of those that should have helped him, it would be all too late. He read and he reasoned. But when he left his study late that evening, worn with the strain of work, the sheet of foolscap was still untouched on his desk. He had not even found a text.

And Saturday came, the day on which he always prepared his sermons, and he sat in his study all the morning. And at first he thought of Hetley, and the Bishop, and Perkin, trying to reason out the advice they would have given him if they had not all failed him, for on that morning he still turned a little to his desire for help, though that desire was no more than a memory now. Perkin he dismissed first from his mind, for it was sound logic and clear convincing argument that he needed now; and there was none of that in Perkin. What books would Hetley recommend, he wondered? What line of reasoning would the Bishop suggest? But soon he put these phantoms of help away

---

[1] Euclid (c. 300 BC) was an ancient Greek mathematician considered the "father of geometry" and chiefly known for his *Elements* treatise, which established the foundations of geometry.

[2] Thomas Babington Macaulay (1800–1859) was an English historian, poet, and politician best known for his extensive and influential 1848 book *The History of England.*

ch. ends next p.

and turned solely to his own energies. In such a crisis, and to such self-reliance, Fortune surely should have come. But she was far away that day, perhaps helping a child to find a lost toy boat in some reeds, too busy to aid this lone champion of Christianity; and the incisive argument, the instances delved out of history, came never upon the foolscap.

The Struggle

And Sunday came, and his bells were ringing as the vicar went to church, ringing and beating back from the walls of the houses, as though their influence pouring from the tall tower of flint had flooded all the valley. It was all as it had been Sunday after Sunday since ever Anwrel knew Wolding; as it had been times out of mind. In those mellow notes all that was lovely in old years seemed to linger, like bright dust that time had frayed from some golden filigree,[1] caught in the cobwebs of a deserted house and held there still when all other gold was gone. Through that ancient triumphing melody, to which even bricks and slates were answering clearly, no sound of any pipes could come, thought the vicar; and new hopes, whose roots were in the echoing music, rose in him suddenly. Yet still he had no text, no telling argument, not a word of his sermon.

He had brought with him the notes of a sermon made two or three years ago, when a thunderstorm had kept all away from the church except five or six, and those few had barely heard it amongst the peals of the thunder: Augusta had reminded

[1] Delicate and intricate ornamental work of fine twisted wire.

him of it and knew where to find the notes. It was a kindly, friendly, human little sermon, and, in face of the trouble that threatened Wolding now, perfectly useless; as Augusta knew; but she knew that he must still preach to the very last, until the end whose approaching shadow she felt, though what it would be she knew not.

So he went into the vestry with his notes, no better equipped to deal with what confronted him than would a soldier be that should attack with a butterfly-net.

All through the service moods passed through his mind, so that sometimes, when he saw that the pews were full, as far as he could discern down the long dim aisle, he believed that the just cause held his people yet; and sometimes despairs with all their terrible certainly assured him that they only drifted there, driven idly by custom, as in parishes that he had heard of folk came to service still, whose faith had withered long since and only habit remained to them.

But when he went up into the pulpit and spread out his notes, and looked up from them at the families he had known so long and well, and saw in their faces as they watched him lines made by sorrows and mirths in which he had had his share, then all those moods departed and only a pity was left to him, so deep that he knew if he spoke it would all well over in tears. So he stood silent, fumbling his useless notes. And then he said: "Oh, my people."

For a moment more he held back the words that were coming, breaking loose under that great pity, as frozen streams pour down at last, in the warmth of some sudden Spring. For he must give them a text. But he had no text to give them. So he quoted part of a sentence from memory out of the prayer-book. "In their time, and in the old time before them." And whatever meaning the incomplete words may have lacked, they carried his own thoughts back, as though by a little golden bridge thrown far over troubled years, to the quieter days of which he would speak with them. And he spoke to them of their own gardens, of lanes they knew and the hedges all white at the end of May, the wild rose in the midst of the year, then the hazel nuts on the uplands, and the journey that the stream made all the while, going quietly on through Wolding like the ages, the stream on whose banks the white-haired farmers there had all sat once on a time angling for minnows. By easy ways and by paths that they all loved he drew them surely back to the old time. The old ways were best, he said, the faith of their fathers and of the old time before them. He told them how the moss came over gravestones like a visible benediction; he told them where first the anemones stole out in the early Spring, and where the hyacinths rioted, and where the old bonfire had been long ago on the hill: these were his arguments, these his allusions from history. And as no arguments would ever have dragged them, so these simple memories led them, till their thoughts were far away with the old time. Were not those days best, he asked them. And before their minds had time to make any comparison their hearts had all answered him. He appealed to them without any rhetoric, and making use of no learning; he stretched out his hands and appealed to them to abide by the old ways. And a hush came down on the simple people of Wolding, like the hush of those who were living now in their memories. Insects that glittered in the streaming sunlight beyond the open door could be heard through the silence singing their own small song. And in that silence at last Augusta hoped.

And now the very thoughts in the vicar's heart were hand in hand with their thoughts, and in sunny gardens of the old lost years their memories went where he led them. Go back through those years, he said, as far as they would in memory, and they would find the old faith still blessing them. What would guide them, he asked them, in the days to come, with all their unseen troubles and unguessed changes, if they deserted the light that had led them so long. Not a dress rustled, not a child stirred or sighed. Softly at first, soft as Spring coming to meadows, soft as birds heard far off by children at play, and strange as the music of ice that the noon and a wind have broken, the sound of pipes rose slowly above the words of the preacher.

Nobody doubted that it was Tommy Duffin: they could hear his hob-nailed boots on the square red tiles that paved the path through the churchyard.

He was playing louder now. The first notes had come like the beckoning of a hand, or like a call in a whisper. But the music was rising now like a conqueror's trumpet, who blows at the borders of an unknown land, calling his followers on. A moment ago and their thoughts had been all about Anwrel, leading them back into the calm of the past, among things no stranger than the glow of old hollyhocks, at the end of the gloaming gathering the last of the light, or than hawkmoths darting silently out of space to poise themselves upon air by a bell-mouthed flower, or than the simple wonder of may. But wonders of which he knew nothing were luring them now; and if the music of those pipes were beating from shores that no learning of his had ever touched, and from regions beyond his dreaming, what hope could there be for those poor simple folk to know where they were going before it was all too late? Too late! At such a thought he faltered, and even paused for a while. In the pause the pipes played on. Then stillness outside the church and stillness in it, and they heard Tommy Duffin's boots as he marched away.

The Battle is Lost and Won

Augusta looked up at the vicar, but he did not need that glance: it was the hour of his effort. If he should fail them now, if they should lose the faith to roam after pagan fantasies, he would be like a shepherd that could not make hurdles upon old wolf-haunted downs. They should not stray, these simple people committed to his charge; he would hold them yet.

There was a stir in the church; heads were turned round away from him; a half-witted boy stole out.

By some movement of his hands he called back their wandering glances. By some tone in his voice he held them, by that ring as he spoke that was like an echo of triumph heard faintly in the voices of the just, rejoicing in happy ardours far from our sphere, and unburdened by our perplexities or only remembering them dreamily. Whatever it was, whenever that rare elation, he knew it when it came, knew that from all the wide and mysterious region of thought his utmost powers were gathering now to help him. It was as it should be; his greatest effort was now; he would win this struggle with all the might that was in him, or fail as forlorn hopes fail, because the last blow is spent and the enemy was the stronger. Thus he spoke to them in his power: thus he appealed to them still.

And again he led their thoughts to the olden years; again he awoke from their sleep or gathered back from their straying, the memories that were living amongst this people of his, illuminating days that had now no other light. He showed them how all the little things they had loved had been guided each to its place in the valleys of Wolding by the old faith of their fathers. Not a lawn they knew, not a rose on a cottage wall, could have come down the years to them without that guidance. The old ways had them in their holding yet. He besought them not to turn away from that guidance after things that were evil and new. And all the while that he besought them he mourned lest through fault of his, through any weakness of reasoning, through any word unsaid, these neighbours of his that he looked upon as his children should stray away far from salvation. He mourned as he spoke, and they felt his sorrow throbbing from every word, vibrating along his sentences, his fear lest because of him this evil should fall on them. He found no fault with them: the fault would all be his, if the good that he had preached to them all these years should be suddenly lost to them utterly. He blamed them no more than a shepherd blames his sheep. And always he turned back to the bygone years; for the faith and the ancient ways were one to him, and were like a garden glowing in soft light, safely fenced from all the cares that perplex our days. He never can have reflected that it was out of those bygone years that the rites of Pan had reached them as well as the Faith, going down time together, as butterfly and pursuing bird go down the same wind. And they recked[1] little of that, for their imaginations did not reach so far as the origin of anything (if, indeed, any human imagination can), and it was only a fight in their minds between the memory of Wolding as Anwrel pictured it, long ago, as the elders knew it, a village whose ways seemed somehow turned toward

---

[1] Took heed or caution.

blessings as its hills sloped to the sunlight, and the memory of that music that all had heard just now, barely ten yards away from the very door. Which memory would hold them? Echoes in the high rafters had scarcely ceased to mutter of that strange music, while the other memory lived in the vicar's voice. And now they seemed turning back to that memory, for it was upon their heartstrings that he was playing, with his strong voice like a violinist's bow. And, as they seemed to turn to him, he told them the story of Wolding through the last generation, the unwritten chronicles of a village of which History had never known. No scholar could have preached to them of any victorious city, or of the glories or learning of any noble age, as he preached to this people of the affairs of Wolding; for he had known all their sorrows, and many a tiny joy, as well as the larger rejoicings when all the village kept holiday. And over all that trivial chronicle as he told it; as though it were gleaming upon every word, or as though the sound of his words broke all the while through the glow of it, hung the old faith, like the gloaming above the valley in summer. Now, with their faces all turned to him, now with his words amongst their inmost thoughts that they thought alone to themselves, sitting late by the fire in winter, he besought them yet again, then stood for a moment gazing silently into their faces. A handkerchief was drawn quietly out in a pew, all white against the dark of the Sunday clothes; and two more. Then three young men with their handkerchiefs to their faces, as though their noses were bleeding, walked out of the church. The younger ones saw them and imitated at once. There was a stir in the pews, and two more handkerchiefs were brought flashing out, in preparation for the stale excuse; when Lily rose up from her seat, and, walking along the pew past Mrs. Airland, stood in the aisle. Standing there in the slenderness of youth, with the splendour of her assurance, she lifted her head and glanced once round the church. Mrs. Airland in the first seat by the aisle was sitting beside her while she stood for that proud moment: she reached out a hand toward the girl to detain her, but the hand driven by an aged uncertain impulse barely reached Lily's dress and gripped nothing. Then Lily walked down the aisle like the bride of a toreador,[2] leaving a bullring still resounding with cheers, like a fairy queen stepping at moonrise out of a forest to pursue some magical thing that her forces had routed, like a royal priestess newly initiated in mysteries to be fathomed alone by her. If the way of a step and the poise of a head can hint such things as these, Lily hinted them as she went, to wondering imaginations.

"Lily," gasped Mrs. Airland when she found her hand had not held her, "that is not the way to go out of church."

But then the thought of that time called Mrs. Airland; not exactly the actual notes of it, but Wold Hill suddenly hallowed by that strange music, and glowing a long way off, deep green with blue shadows, under a haze of gold of that very tint that had seemed to hang between Earth and the fairy hills of tales that were told to her when she was very young. And Wold Hill seemed to call her to come at once, and to leave her pony-trap[3] that would be waiting outside, and to go straight up the slope, not by the slanting path that led to her house, but right to the woods and over the top of the hill; and to go blithely,[4] as she would have gone long ago, forgetting many years, and everything but that music.

Young men and girls were streaming out of the church, with no more pretences now that Lily had gone.

The vicar paused, and there was only the sound of feet. He glanced at Mrs. Airland, seeming to hope that her example might stay some, and that he could yet preach on to a little group.

Mrs. Airland was putting her things together tidily, her prayer-book and hymnbook, small handbag and parasol.[5] Then she muttered aloud: "It seems a long while ago." And

---

[2] Bullfighter.
[3] Pony-drawn carriage.
[4] In a happy, carefree manner.
[5] A light umbrella used as a sunshade.

nobody that heard her knew quite what she meant. Then the old neat figure rose up, and walked trimly away.

Anwrel preached on. He did not appeal to them now to remember old gardens, lit by gloamings of long ago, gladdening the last few years of folk that this congregation had known, sleeping now, outside, in the faith, under huge yew trees. There are aphorisms, quotations, maxims and phrases, common to many a sermon preached by men whose honest hearts were made without one ingredient of oratory. Anwrel knew, now, he had failed. Nothing remained for him but to preach on still. So he preached the old aphorisms, the smooth-worn sayings, to the last of his congregation as their heels rapped down the aisles. With resolute mastery that held down the tears in his voice he preached them the thin bare phrases whose texture had once held thought. He preached on till all seemed gone, all but Augusta. She alone. In such a defeat her steadfastness barely brought comfort to him.

Now it was time to end. So he gathered together his poor sentences, and rounded them to some kind of conclusion, while only Augusta listened.

The last word of his sermon was said; and, as he said it, before he turned round to the East for the dedicatory conclusion, Augusta got up from her seat and followed the rest.

31

The Woods of Apple

Then Anwrel glanced once all round the church and saw no one, and turned to the East in the silence as Augusta's steps hurried away, and said the final words. As he said the amen that completely concluded his sermon, there came from the shadows of pillars at the dim end of the church a clear voice saying approvingly:

"Very good. Very good."

For the space of a moment Anwrel stood perfectly still; then, coming down from his pulpit, saw past a pillar, and there was Perkin, alone in the furthest pew, sitting leaning forward with both hands clasped on his stick. The lonely vicar ran down the aisle toward him. "Perkin," he said.

"Yes," said Perkin. "Very good."

"But they would not hear me. They have all gone. I have failed," said Anwrel.

"Hist," said Perkin. "Not yet."

"But they're gone," said Anwrel. "Gone away to the hill. Even . . ." But he could not say it.

"Yes. All gone," said Perkin in his rich voice, with eyes twinkling.

"Oh, why did you not come sooner?" cried the vicar.

"There were forces opposed to that journey of which this world knows nothing."

"How did you come?" asked the vicar.

"I overcame them," said Perkin.

And the vicar at that moment of such complete failure could do no more than repeat, "Oh, why did you not come sooner?"

"Why! But you're doing famously," said Perkin. "A very good sermon."

"But they're all gone," wailed Anwrel.

"You strengthened their illusions well," said Perkin. "And they must have illusions, you know."

"Strengthened them!" exclaimed Anwrel. "They've forsaken everything!"

"That's because the other illusion is stronger," said Perkin.

At this Anwrel groaned.

"Why, yes," said Perkin. "When you strengthened your illusions he had to strengthen his. Didn't you hear his pipes? And so there are better illusions on earth than there were. Very good."

"He? Who?" muttered Anwrel.

"That other fellow you spoke of."

"The enemy. Oh, the enemy," moaned the vicar.

"He has some good illusions," replied Perkin.

But Anwrel without answering led the way to the vestry along one aisle of the deserted church. He feared now he was past the help of even the fertile mind of this curious man, and yet was loath to leave him and face loneliness. As they left the vestry on the way to the vicarage there seemed something in Perkin's mood that was far from despair; and some reflected hope shone faintly on Anwrel, in spite of all that defeat and reason told him.

Again Perkin spoke of illusions.

"You must have some, you know. If you don't, they get to hear of it outside Earth. Aye, and beyond Neptune."

"Then why have you none yourself?" Anwrel blurted out in his bitterness.

"I? Because I can see through all illusions. All but one. And even that one, I know what it is made of. Dust and ashes. All dust and ashes."

So sadly spoke Perkin, that all the bitterness of the taste of defeat, of that deep draught of disappointment, vanished from Anwrel, and all at once he was thinking only of Perkin.

"What illusion was that?" he asked kindly.

"My love for Mary," said the grey wanderer. Anwrel laid a hand on his shoulder.

"No love such as that," he said, for he saw it clearly glowing in the deep eyes, "no great love, none, can be dust and ashes ever."

"Wrong there, parson. Wrong there," said Perkin. "For a parson came, and one a lot older than you, and said those very words. Those were the very words he said over Mary."

Anwrel sighed, and kept his hand on the wanderer's shoulder.

"Yes," the old man went on, "and before that all things had meanings, but they all joined up into one meaning. Now they only have meanings; each one by itself. All separate, all separate; ever since the parson said those words over Mary."

And still Anwrel could do nothing but grip the old man's shoulder as he walked in silence beside him, hearing those broken words thrown up from the storm of an old sorrow.

"And I'm always glad to help a parson," the wanderer went on, "for I never bore him a grudge for what he said. It was true enough, true enough. Mary is dust and ashes."

Then they walked for a while both silent. And then Anwrel sighed and said: "But you won't believe in our Heaven."

"Not believe in it! Not believe in it!" said Perkin. "Why, I was there last night."

"You were there?" gasped Anwrel.

"Yes, I couldn't sleep. Things wouldn't let me be. Small troubles roaming the air, that vex folk without reason. They were skipping and hovering foolishly over Seldham, and they wouldn't let me be. And then, just as I thought I was getting to sleep at last, just as I was going off, my spirit started wandering. So there was no more sleep for me that night."

"And then?" said the vicar, for Perkin had stopped and seemed going to say no more.

"I wandered and wandered," said Perkin. "And, oh, then I came to Heaven."

"How did you know?" asked the vicar.

"Well, first of all, you could see it wasn't Earth. The colours alone, you know."

"More intense, I suppose," said the vicar.

"Hills on Earth are bluish sometimes," continued Perkin, "but not sheer bright blue. And then there were the prayers wobbling up in faint gold streaks, and sounding like violins."

"Could you hear the words?" asked the vicar.

"Words? No," said Perkin.

"How did you know they were prayers?"

"The tone of them," said Perkin. "They couldn't have been anything else."

"What was it like?" asked the vicar.

"I was in a wood."

"What trees?" asked the vicar.

"Apple."

"Yes."

"And I could see the far hills shining through the wood, bright blue as I said. And angels were there with great gold haloes on, like harvest moons rising and rising up through the wood. And St. Ethelbruda was playing amongst the angels."

"How did you know it was her?" the vicar asked.

"We all know her in these parts," said Perkin.

"Yes," said the vicar. "Go on."

"She was playing amongst the angels," Perkin continued.

"What were they playing at?" the vicar asked. For he had a trust in this wandering man that he would have given to his bishop, or to the learning of Hetley, but all had deserted him except this one strange man.

And Perkin answered him: "There was a wind blowing from Earth, with a touch of sharpness in it that nearly shrivelled the prayers but could not hurt the blossoms of that wood."

"How could cold reach Heaven from here?" the vicar asked, anxious to learn what he could from that wandering spirit that had seen the land of which he had taught so long.

"It wasn't cold," said the wanderer. "It was jealousy."

"Jealousy!" exclaimed the vicar. "That cannot ever touch the angels."

"No," explained Perkin. "They were playing at it."

"Playing at it?"

"Yes, they were leaning toward that wind blowing out of Earth, and remembering tiny things and mundane ways, and toying with earthly emotions, and trying to remember what they would have felt in our fields, centuries since, in jealousy of the sanctity and the miracles of Ethelbruda, had jealousy been possible to them. That is what they were playing at."

The vicar was silent a moment. Then he said, "I do not doubt your word; but I think you must be mistaken in what you saw. Angels and blessed spirits could never be so trivial."

"There's *nothing* so volatile as an angel," shouted the wanderer. "Upon any mere whim of righteousness, or fancy of charity, their spirits will float for hours. And, as for being mistaken, they are more transparent than gossamer. They were playing at jealousy; and probably had been for ages. For, you know, she does work miracles; and they had been holy for ages before she was heard of, yet they've never been able to do a half of what she can. Not a half of it. There was plenty of stuff to play with. They were looking down at our fields and playing at that: and the fields seemed even tinier than jealousy, though they all seem so big here.

"And it never really troubled them, though they felt it blowing from Earth: it would have put their haloes out if it had: one knew that. I told you how it sort of shrivelled the prayers.

"And then as they played, as in my opinion they had been playing for ages (the same game all that time), the wind suddenly ceased. Not a puff to make them remember, not a breath to try in vain to trouble the apple-blossoms. And the angels sat still as wild roses under their harvest moons, with nothing whatever to play at.

"I knew what that was. She's beaten, I said. She can't work miracles any more, and there's not enough left to make jealousy even in play. Who'd beat her, I said? Why, that goat-legged fellow you were speaking of, who was here before her time. And then I thought of you, and I left Heaven, and I came on here at once. He'll want me now, I said."

"Thank you," said Anwrel. "Thank you."

And they walked on then in silence and so came to his empty home.

Perkin Seeks an Illusion

Anwrel, seeking at first helplessly and even despairingly in cupboards and along shelves, came at last on bread, cheese, and butter, and part of a cold chicken. And soon he and his strange companion were sitting at dinner in the deserted house, and now a little of his despair was lifting from the vicar, rest and quiet and food all having their share in this; but chiefly that slight lifting, like one wisp of mist swirling away from a shrouded field, was caused by his trust in Perkin. He had recognised from the first the strong far-travelling mind, while others saw only the cut of his clothes and hat; and from the very first Perkin had come to him when all others deserted. He had reason enough to trust him with all his intuitions. But now plodding after those intuitions, as it ever plods behind, came logic to approve the trust he had felt. For, however Perkin had gone, he had come back from wherever he went with definite information that the vicar himself could corroborate, though it came from far beyond the confines of Earth and outside the scope of time: St. Ethelbruda could no longer work miracles.

Could anyone have told him, thought the vicar? Who would tell such things to Perkin? Who would talk at all to that crazed wanderer? No, that was impossible. But the angels: they could have told him, or spirits of the blessed. It was clear that his mind was perpetually mazed[1] by spirits. And was it not to just such as him that the angels were wont to speak, when they spoke to anyone on our earth at all?

"You were right about St. Ethelbruda," he said.

"Right?" said the wanderer. "Didn't I tell you I saw her? And a look on her face pretending to vaunt[2] herself. For such things can only be pretence, where she is. And the angels all round her playing at jealousy. And then the look went out of her face. And I knew she'd no more to boast of even in play."

"Yes, yes," said the vicar. "All true."

The wanderer leaned forward suddenly and gripped the vicar's knee.

"I couldn't have been mistaken," he exclaimed.

"It was good of you to come away," said the vicar. "You might have forgotten me and stopped to see, to see Mary, you know."

"No," said the old wanderer clutching a flap of his coat and thrusting it forward into Anwrel's notice. "Not in this kit.[3] Too far for it."

"Too far?" said the vicar.

"Too far for this outfit," said the wanderer. "She'd be away in one of those cities beyond the wood. Little cities with spires all over the bright blue hills. I might have got there perhaps, if you hadn't wanted me. But I'd never have got back to this old suit if I had. Some day, perhaps. Some day. But not with these boots and bones."

"Ah, dear me," said the vicar, stung by the contrast of all his despairs and perplexities, and the bright blue hills with their spires shining over the apple-blossom, "it is a hard world to come back to."

"World? It's a bin," said the wanderer. "All full of dust and ashes."

---

[1] Dazed and confused.

[2] Excessively praise or boast about.

[3] In this context, clothing used for travel.

A purpose came suddenly into the wanderer's eyes, and he slowly rose from the table. He moved to the door.

"Where are you going?" asked Anwrel.

"Seeking," said Perkin.

"What for?" asked Anwrel.

"The old search," said the wanderer. "Looking for illusions. And this one's taken all your parish away. Who knows? It might hold me yet."

And he spoke with a wistfulness and a quiet that was almost like the tones of one not afflicted by dreams. And he looked through the window at Wold Hill, all shimmering in the sun.

"But what shall I do? What shall I do?" cried Anwrel.

"Why, what does one need but illusions?" answered Perkin.

"They're gone. I've lost them," said the vicar. "One can't hold them all alone." He spread his hands to the emptiness of his room. "I've none to help me now."

"Plenty of friends over there," said Perkin, pointing to Wold Hill. "Plenty of illusions."

"But," gasped Anwrel, "but they're the enemy's!"

"They're yours if you want them," said Perkin.

"What!" cried the vicar.

But the door shut and Perkin was gone.

All alone now. And plenty of time for reflection. But nothing to reflect upon that had not been all worked over and over and found vain. And Perkin, in whom he had trusted so much, who was all he had left to trust to, had given him advice against which his mind was shut: come what may he would not go to Wold Hill, to those unhallowed rites and the heathen stones. Those were the very words that passed through his mind; but underneath them thoughts surged to and fro, a multitude too many and moving too swiftly for the thinker himself to discern them. All the afternoon in the empty house the lonely thoughts raced on. And then, about five o'clock, came a slight sound on the gravel, and a rustling inside the hall: and the door was opened and Augusta walked in.

"I'm so sorry," she said.

But she was not apologising for anything she had done; there was no trace of that in her voice. She was only sorry for him. For herself, she seemed to have slipped from her the weight of all that worry, the burden of which had grown harder day after day, till the lines of her face were all drawn taut with the strain of it. But now the look of strain in her face had gone, and she looked composed at last, as though all the anxiety of those weeks was over.

"Augusta," he said. No other words came to say to her.

"I stayed till you finished," she said.

He looked at her and did not speak; so she spoke instead.

"I thought . . ." she began.

"What did you think?" he said at last.

"I thought you would have come too," she said.

"I?" he asked.

"We all thought so," she answered.

Was everyone and everything driving him to the old stones beyond Wold Hill? He remained silent.

"You wouldn't come?" she asked.

"Never," he said.

"It's almost a pity," she said.

"A pity!" exclaimed Anwrel.

"Only," she said, "because they were thinking of sacrificing a bull. And you would have done it so well."

He looked round at the walls of the room with their little religious prints, and their secular ornaments upon velvet-hung brackets, so hallowed by fashion in such myriad homes, that these secular knick-knacks were now as ritual as the religious. Yes, it was the walls of a vicarage, amidst which such words were said to him!

"They are going to get Mudden to do it if you don't come," she said. "And he's not the man for a thing like that. One doesn't want only a butcher."

And as she said this she went over and rang the bell. "We'll have some tea," she added.

"It's no use ringing," he said. "There's no one there."

ch. ends next p.

"Oh, they're all back now," she said.

Well, Pan had won, thought the vicar. But there was one that he had not taken captive yet. He would hold out alone.

But what good would that do?

And there came over him the loneliness of surrounded men, that fight on still and know that their cause is lost.

33
The Smile of the Palaeolith

Augusta and the vicar said little that evening. The vicar sat grave with thought; while Augusta seemed waiting for him to come to some decision, a decision that she seemed expecting to hear at any moment, and that somehow seemed to be clear enough in her mind.

Yet what could he do? If he were not a parson he might have taken Augusta seriously when she spoke so strangely about a bull: he might have followed Perkin's advice and abandoned his lonely struggle and found happiness again amongst his fellow-men, listening to music whose magic had entranced him already as much as any of them.

There was no longer any strain in Augusta's face; no perplexities left any mark there.

How could things seem so simple to Augusta? The slightest shadow of the embarrassment caused by their silence lay at times across her expression, but no sign of any worry. How could things be so clear to her while to him they remained so intricate as to show no right path for him through the mazes of the dark future?

Supper came, and still she said little, still waiting for that simple statement from him, when there was nothing simple to say. And he sat dark with his thoughts.

They went to bed; and all Anwrel's despairs and failures rocked his mind to sleep almost at once; so that, lulled by this kindness of the mercy of Nature, he never heard the pipes, some while after midnight, when a waning moon rose. Strange steps had entered his dreams, leading him over the Wold in a walk back through the centuries, enriching his dreams with wonders far beyond the learning of Hetley; but nothing had awoken the weary man. And it was not till an hour later that he awoke, and found Augusta was gone. He called her loudly, he impulsively pulled the bell; but the echoes of his own voice and the bell's tinkle only gave emphasis to the hush of the house.

Again he was all alone.

He felt he must think. His mind was all fresh from sleep. But thinking told him nothing but that he had been thinking for weeks, and it had brought him no help yet. Then he must try action, a thing often vaguely praised. But what was he to do?

An uneasy feeling of darkness, solitariness, and magic was hurrying him: but whither?

Well, first of all he must dress. So he dressed, still not knowing what he was going to do.

Then he went downstairs carrying a bedroom candle, and found his broad-brimmed hat hanging up in the hall. But perhaps he could think better in his study.

So he went in there with his candle.

He walked round the little room anxiously, as though any material thing he could find there could possibly help his thoughts.

Something about the freedom with which echoes of creaks of boards went soaring away triumphantly through the house seemed to tell him that the whole vicarage was empty.

Ornaments, furniture, pictures, one by one, came into his earnest gaze as the candle-flame passed them. And suddenly the old palaeolith.

It almost looked up at the candle. If two inanimate things

could greet each other, then that streaming flame bringing sudden colour and shape to the formless things huddled up in the dark of the night greeted the grim old axe that smiled back at once, with shadows shifting among its flinty hollows.

If the old stone grinned at the vicar with those shadows astir in its hollows, he was in just the state to see it and to interpret its meaning, for anxiety had so sharpened his nerves that they did not miss things like that. He looked at the stone once more, bending slightly toward it. And the movement of his head moved his hand and the candle, and the little shadows that lay on the stone all flickered and changed again. This time he felt it had winked at him.

Toward this moment everything had been trending. He saw that now. The Bishop's refusal of help; his sending of Hetley to Wolding, the one man who must for certain be utterly useless, because he could not hear; the desertion of him by all that were sane and practical, till only Perkin was left to him: all, all these things had conspired to leave him helpless at last, amongst primitive things as far from civilization as little things lost by the sea at the height of its tide are far from their home at the ebb. Yes, he seemed back with all Wolding in the days of such weapons as this; and it felt to him as if thousands of years must roll over the world again before anything could return of the faith he had tried to preach. His hand shook at the thought, and the moving shadows made the smile of the flint seem grim at this sign of his weakening.

What should he do? What did the great flint want? Perhaps the Old Stones knew. He must go to the Old Stones.

He would take the palaeolith. How carry it? Queer memories came to the tired mind from the flint, that a mind not frayed now by anxieties would never have felt at all, queer memories of how the old axe liked to be carried.

He had a great thick stick that he used to take when he went on his walks over the hills. He went and found it now. Next he needed strips of hide, and remembered an old pair of leggings. With a good sharp knife that he had he cut a strip from the legging, carefully turning when he got to the end, and going back again and again, till it was all in one long strip. And with this he bound the grim old axe to the wood. When he had done this he extinguished his candle and slipped quietly out of the house.

The night outside was wonderfully blackened by the old trees that clustered about the vicarage and leaned over all its paths. And for a while the vicar had nothing to guide him but the pale surface of the drive. When this reached the road trees were fewer, and there were stars to be seen; and already the vicar's eyes, finding their master roaming the open night, were beginning to fit themselves for their new guidance. The cold of the hour, that was about him when he started, increased with the chill of the valley; for though it was only a tiny stream that sparkled through Wolding, and seemed to add by its brightness to the warmth of the sun-drenched slopes, yet at night a power seemed to arise from the stream and to grip the whole valley. Through the chill of this grip the vicar went down the road, and through the long hush of the village, and came to the bridge that went over the stream at a shallow.

By this very way the old flint that he carried must often have come before; for the ford by the little bridge where the carts drove through today would have been the ford always; and the street by which the vicar had come through the village and the track that joined it, going up Wold Hill and straight for the Old Stones, must have been a pathway from hill to hill far back in the days that shaped us, in the days none knew, and that very few thought mattered.

The vicar crossed the bridge and went up the slope by the way that led over the hill to the Old Stones, the night seeming friendlier to him than ever it had before, for the sake, as it almost seemed, of the primitive thing that he carried.

And, had any watched in the empty village then, he had seen an English parson at the close of the nineteenth century, going furtively through the night, and carrying with a certain primeval dignity an axehead that no doubt had played its part while the victory of Man over other creatures trembled still in the balance and none knew yet who would rule the world in the end.

34
The Blood on the Long Flat Stone

The pipes that had summoned Mrs. Anwrel that night had summoned all the village, and they were all sitting there a dark circle about the Old Stones. This was to be the night, they had been told that afternoon by Tommy Duffin. It ought really to have been on midsummer's eve,[1] he said, but it was to be tonight instead. And they all came: they felt that they knew now, since they had forsaken the ways of the 19th century finally that afternoon (and, for that matter, the ways of the last 2000 years), that it was wrong to resist the call of those pipes of reed. They had all gone over the hill to the Old Stones a little while after midnight. They were all there: Lily crowned with a wreath of moss roses, that seemed to have come from Mrs. Airland's garden, from an old red wall looking South; and, respectfully further away from the long flat stone, Mrs. Airland herself; and Mrs. Anwrel, seated quietly on the ground, as though she rested from wondering; and Mrs. Duffin, resting from telling stories of the seventeen years of the life of her son Tommy, because this

[1] Midsummer, or the summer solstice, is traditionally on or about June 21 in the Northern Hemisphere.

was not the occasion for talk; and Mr. Duffin holding tight to his attitude that he would never have been surprised at Tommy doing something of the sort, on account of the aptitude he had often shown for one thing and another; and Willie Latten with his band of young men standing, armed each with a stick, in a circle in front of the seated villagers, as though they were an escort to the Old Stones of Wolding; and Skegland, utterly forgetting his groceries; and Marion, the maid from the vicarage, forgetting her young man in Yorkshire; and Mrs. Tweedy, forgetting everything; and Latten the carpenter and Mrs. Latten, and Hibbuts and Spelkins, and Blegg, and Mrs. Datchery and Mrs. Tichener: in fact all except four young men who had gone away to a farm in a valley beyond the one of the Old Stones, and for whose return all were waiting, while Tommy Duffin stood silent by the flat stone. And near him, but outside the circle of stones, waited Mudden, the butcher, with his great killing hammer.

A small flame burned airily in the midst of the central stone.

In a hush that a whisper stirred, or an owl's hoot rent[2] like a scream, they heard a scuffle in the valley of the Old Stones, below them, further from Wolding; and they turned their heads all together, with the sound of one rustling. It was the four young men bringing up the bull from the farm.

The grey circle of villagers sitting in the dark never moved, except where a few rose up to make way for the roped bull. He was brought through the circle, and through the circle of stones, reluctant but not alarmed, but then he suddenly snorted: when he saw the long flat stone it seemed that the bull knew.

As they dragged the bull gradually forward Tommy Duffin lifted the pipes with the suddenness of a strange thought, and played a tune he had never played before. The whites of the bull's eyes showed in the dark at the sound of it, as though that music had carried him some clear message. All the villagers rose at the music.

---

[2] Disturbed with a shrill or piercing tone.

Mudden, with his great hammer, stepped into the circle of stones.

"No, it must be at dawn," said Tommy Duffin. Then he resumed his piping.

The principal marvel of that music seemed to be that it could enchant old memories, long, long since dead you had fancied, and bring them out of a time you thought utterly buried, and set them living in minds that had known them never, and had barely guessed them in dreams. This music held the people of Wolding tranced by the Old Stones; the carpenter, the sexton, the grocer, Mrs. Airland and all the rest; and not only them it seemed, for there were more than one or two that were there that night who fancied a stir in the wood, a sound like the moving of something gigantic but stealthy, as though some mystery had scented the blood of the bull and been lured through space and through time by a greed for sacrifice. Such thoughts are only guesses: too little was seen for anyone to be sure. But certainly the echoes of Tommy's music grew stronger not weaker, going from hill to hill; and increased, and did not lose, their beauty and wonder, beating against the wood; and swelled to a melody that never yet had come from Tommy's pipes, leaving him gasping, while the echoes rang on and on. And tears welled up in them all, salt and hot, but they saw through the gold of them that they and the distant stars, and the little lives near in the wood, and the Earth and its rocks and its flowers, were not separate as they had thought; and how this was they all knew well while that music played, but they have all forgotten it now. And some say they saw a dark shape larger than man's, in the wood a little above them, playing this music of which the hills and the woods seemed made, and some could not pick it out from the dusk and the branches of trees. But Mrs. Tichener, whose eyes had got queer of late, but who could see better and better the further away things were, called out "It's that there Reverend Davidson."

And in that moment some wandering ray, the first of the gleams of dawn, slipped from under the rim of the world and defeated the stars. They all paled, and darkness paled as well as the light, and the mysteries of night were over. All looked for that shape in the dusk to which the old woman had pointed, and at first they all saw nothing; and then, coming down through the wood, empty now of immortal shapes, whom should they see but the vicar with his stone axe!

Nobody spoke. It seemed to them so right that the vicar should come just now, with that flint axe, just before dawn, that they merely made way for him in silence where their ring was nearest the wood; and he walked on through the circle of them and came near to the Old Stones. Augusta just looked up at him and smiled.

The impulse that had driven the vicar with his axe across the valley to that grey circle of stones, had brought him there and had done its work. He had some leisure at last for reason. In one swift glance he saw all, from the axe in his hand to the bull, and the flame on the altar, going paler and paler with every hint of the dawn. He saw now for what he had come. And, as clearly as he saw his old congregation in the pale but growing light, he saw his own motive in coming. Many thoughts band together to drive a perplexed man, and not all in the same way; but that great flint axe that he carried to that ancient circle of stones was clearer to see than any thought to remember; this alone was clear and conclusive, and stood up amongst the vague thoughts of many days, revealing his own course to him, as the rocky head of a cliff may rise above mist, showing the way to land. Yes, he had come for this. To sacrifice unto heathen gods, in the midst of these heathen stones, before all his congregation.

At such a moment, or, if that be impossible, on the threshold of much lesser errors, a clergyman thinks of his bishop. Anwrel thought of his bishop now. And he thought of him almost with fury. A fight, as he looked back now over all these weeks, had been fought by himself alone, a fight utterly vital to the Church, and one such as she had not had to contend in since the very earliest centuries. With any support he could have won. Had the whole bench of bishops come to Wolding, the poor man thought, it would not have been undue force to have employed in such a crisis. And what had happened? His own bishop by kindness, by tact, and by superior ability had merely avoided a scandal. Upon that alone he had concentrated.

Then learning had failed him in Hetley. Then all that was busy and practical, in Porton. Then Heaven and Earth. He knew not which of these last had been the bitterer blow, Heaven, when Ethelbruda failed him, or Earth, when all the simple folk that he loved had gone out of his church and over the hill to the enemy. He thought of Ethelbruda the more bitterly: only a woman after all, he thought; piqued because the enemy had reappeared, and with some success, in the land wherein she had been hitherto so victorious. But the heavier blow he had suffered had been the blow from Earth.

Well, he was all alone now. Toward this all things had drifted him. None had held him back. He had resisted against everything. And now?

Only the martyrs would have held out longer.

Tommy played again softly by the long flat stone. The bull was restless. The flame on the altar grew paler and paler, till it gave rather colour than light. And colour was coming back everywhere. A blackbird began to sing; and everybody was waiting.

At this last moment when he was throwing over everything, and all the meaning of the work of his life, a compassion for the bull held him back. He went up to Tommy Duffin by the long stone.

"Couldn't we, perhaps . . . " he began diffidently, looking towards the bull.

But Mudden came up to him, seeing what he would say.

"It's an old bull, sir," said Mudden. "He's been kept back for this."

And when nothing whatever seemed to hold him back any longer from sacrificing to gods against whom he had fought, the vicar went up to the stone and stood there waiting for dawn. And they brought the bull nearer.

All the congregation looked at his axe as the vicar stood there waiting, and all knew that it was right it should be of flint, and that Mudden's iron weapon would never do. Anwrel felt their approval of it.

He knew that the sacrifice should be at dawn. He knew this from something that Tommy's pipes seemed to be saying. There should be blood on the long flat stone for the sun to see. And it should be new at sunrise, so that Those who cared for blood should snuff its savour, going up from the freshness of Earth with the first of the odours of morning.

There was a dip in the downs through which the rising sun might have shone on the stones, and indeed did shine on them on midsummer's day some thousands of years ago, but a wood had grown up there since those days. In any case there is a certain slow wobble about our old Earth as she spins, and it had shifted the dip in the downs a little away from the East. Also it was now long past midsummer's day.

So the vicar, seeing there would be no sun on the stone at the exact moment of dawn, waited instead until he felt the expectancy of his congregation well up to a certain height. Then he signed and the bull was brought forward. (In later years they cut the trees, and held that ceremony at the proper hour and on the correct day. This was only their first sacrifice.)

There slept along Anwrel's arms, and were not yet withered, muscles with which he had rowed when thirty years younger. With these he swung the axe as the bull came up to the stone. He aimed at a large white patch on the bull's forehead, below the thickness of horn; and struck the patch where he aimed; and the stick and the leather thong held, and the grim edge of the flint, that it had been given so many ages ago, and the great skull crumpled in and the bull jumped forward, and fell twitching over the stone. They cut its throat, and the long flat stone had blood again, if only the blood of a bull. And an exhilaration seemed to thrill through the palaeolith after a thirst of ages. Tommy Duffin's pipes played on, telling the dawn what they had done in Wolding; and faint and from far

ch. ends next p.

off hills came echoes again, beyond words or imagination: if words can hint, at all, those echoes' elusive meaning they told of triumph or taunt; perhaps taunting, if they dared to fare so far as the fields of Heaven, perhaps taunting St. Ethelbruda. But of what rivalries there may be among immortal powers we may never know anything, and of what music hints we can never do more than guess; only on the firmer ground of mortal sorrows, and of mortal disappointments and of their fading at last, can we even hope to speak surely. No one in Wolding had had so much to bear, as the vicar during the months of his lonely fight: disappointments succeeding each other had made the fight harder and harder, until there were no more disappointments left to come, and he still fought on alone. Now the fight was over for him. Great dignitaries of the Church might take it up, and St. Ethelbruda might succour[3] them. But it was over for him. And with his rest from that long struggle against his parishioners the great weight of his loneliness lifted. And a cheery voice came chuckling out of the crowd:

"All right now, sir. Aren't you?"

And Perkin came forward with a hand held out, to congratulate him on having found an illusion.

---

[3] Assist or give aid.

35
The Return of the Wild

So ended the surge and tumult of those troubles, at war with the rapid host of a myriad thoughts, whose battlefield was the quiet of a clergyman's mind. Nothing remains of those sorrows and agitations, that are more real to any mind in trouble than ought that the eye can see; not even a furrow in Anwrel's cheery face seems to hint them to the observant. Nothing remains for me now to tell of but visible things.

The village adhered to their worship at the Old Stones. Every midsummer's day at dawn they sacrificed there, pouring the blood of a bull all over the long flat stone, that the savour of the blood might go up on first airs of the sunniest day, to be snuffed by whatever might lurk in the vast space of man's ignorance.

Other rites too they held there. There, both crowned with roses from Mrs. Airland's garden, and garlanded with wild thyme, Lily and Tommy were wed one summer's evening according to the rites of Pan. Some rumour of it strayed beyond the valley, and caused pain in certain quarters, and was fortunately soon hushed up. Indeed the listless content of the villagers, and the very able handling of their case, whenever there was risk of its causing attention, soon shut any news of them off from the places that matter; and the wider interests, the affairs of moment, soon went their way without them.

Tommy remained their druid, their priest or inspirer, whatever be the right word: they merely called him the Piper.

After a while the Bishop, with the consent of Convocation in Arches, and the approval of the Dean of Closes,[1] amalgamated the parish with that of Hooton-on-Uplands. And it was understood that the Rector of Hooton should ask his curate to go to Wolding; "to run over to Wolding" were the exact words, for the arrangement was purely informal; in order to hold a service there at any time that might seem needful, indeed at any time at all. Anwrel was not unfrocked.[2] It was felt, well, it was felt that such extreme action should only be taken in cases that merited such a measure. For some while he lived on at the vicarage. Then he and Augusta built themselves a hut nearer to Wold Hill, so as to be more amongst the people that were all the world to them.

A wonderful quiet, a quiet you could feel if you ever strayed that way, some fragment of the quiet that the world had lost, came down upon Wolding. Tommy Duffin's curious music that lured one away from the present, and that then seemed to wake up old memories that nobody guessed were there, seems to have come at a time when something sleeping within us first guessed that the way by which we were then progressing toward the noise of machinery and the clamour of sellers, amidst which we live today, was a wearying way, and they turned from it. And turning from it they turned away from the folk that were beginning to live as we do.

Not a soul saw them outside the valley of Wolding. They had felt that if they did not break away quickly they would never do it at all. So there they lived, and you never saw one of them.

---

[1] Likely an allusion to the real Court of Arches, presided over by the Dean of Arches, an ecclesiastical court of the Church of England covering the Province of Canterbury, named for the street-level arched windows of the old crypt of St Mary-le-Bow where the court still sits.

[2] Defrocked; to be deprived of priestly privileges and functions.

After a fashion they ploughed and sowed. Indeed, had you seen them in the ploughing season, you had not at once seen the difference between them and other men. But birches slipped every year from the edges of woods, and began to grow, at first like fairy children, that you barely saw unless you were looking for magic. Then a few years went by, and there they were standing at the end of a field, with a silvery light on their leaves enchanting the green, and holding that part of the field for what was there before ploughshares.[3] And in a little while you must have seen, had you strayed at all in those fields, that there was a certain neighbourliness permitted to any wild sapling, that showed that no industrious farmers dwelt there. They did not take deliberately to skins and untanned leather, but merely patched old clothes with these things, or whatever came handy, rather than trade with the world beyond, that was changing so fast away from them every year. They worked in a simple way at all the crafts that are necessary, and lived by their agriculture, though the woods were encroaching slowly all the while. For instance a clump of privet[4] dwelt just at the edge of a wood, getting light all day from the South, and had never seemed to spread, so far as anyone noticed; but now it was doubling in size with every few years, and every North wind that blew seemed to carry it further; and when ten or twelve years had gone the fritillaries[5] found it scattered all over the slope, that was once only golden grass in the glint of the sun. And of course the wayfaring tree came too, with its bouquet-like blossoms, and its scarlet berries aflame at the end of the year. In flat fields the plough still held back such encroachments as these, but wherever a difficult slope leaned to the sunlight these things of the wild came back. And even juniper began to appear. And thorn, of course, almost came leaping forward to regain

---

[3] Primary cutting blades of a plow (plough).

[4] A shrub of the olive family, with small white heavily scented flowers and poisonous black berries, commonly grown as a hedge.

[5] In this context, butterflies with orange-brown wings that are checkered with black and silver.

what was lost to the wild for the last few centuries. It would seize a field and dot it with separate bushes, almost as though some wild plan had made the disorderly lines: and the bushes towered upward with none to harm them, till the flash of their green in April added a light to the Earth, and their whiteness in June was a splendour. Among them the nightingales sang all through May, the moment the blackbirds had ended, singing on through the dark till they woke the cuckoo. To such fields the wild clematis came, crawling and clambering, and joining bush to bush, till the place became a thicket too dense for man, and many a little creature could quietly rejoice in deep shadow or sing its triumph in sunlight from some high twig. And not only in upland fields was the wild returning, while man and his ways fell back on straiter defences; but even here and there in the village itself there were apple trees dropping back at the edges of orchards to earlier and wilder memories, becoming more like crabapples year after year; and lilac and laburnum[6] leaned out over walls as though they too would stray away to the wild. And, by walls and by wire and by hedge, everything seemed to be pushing at man's narrowed defences. Walls bulged and leaned awry; wire blackened; wire-netting fell into gaps that the rabbits found; gaps widened, and wire-netting at last would fall in showers, rustling on to dead leaves, if anyone touched it, and handfuls of it could almost be crumpled away. Hedges alone stood strong; but who could say if they were for man or the enemy?

They put up no more wire, for they had none in the village and had no intercourse with the towns beyond: relics of it gripped by old trees, whose trunks had grown against it till they enclosed it, remained to show the lines man had formerly held. Wild roses, once an adornment of the lanes that ran through Wolding, now shone high over them, and curved inward and met, and sank with their own weight, and mixed with new tendrils slowly soaring below, till the mass of briar held the

---

[6] A small Eurasian tree with clusters of bright yellow drooping flowers; all parts of the plant are poisonous.

lanes against man. These and the clematis were slowly closing in Wolding.

Foxes and badgers multiplied. And the whole valley became a draw for the Ulford Hounds.[7] It was soon the surest draw they had in the East Downlands. But in a year or so they gave up coming there. There was something about the people that they found queer. A new member of the Hunt, dining at the Master's house one evening and listening to talk about meets on the next card, as a young member of Parliament might listen to his leader telling plans for the coming session, would say, perhaps: "What about Wolding?"

"Wolding?" the Master would say.

"Yes," says the young man. "It looked a good sort of place."

"Oh, well," says the Master, "I don't think we'll go there."

And, likely as not, no more than that will be said. Or, if the young sportsman has come only lately into the Ulford country, he may ask, "No foxes there?"

"Oh, the foxes are all right," the Master will say.

I have never heard of it being much discussed by any that hunt with the Ulford. Even a direct question to any of them will draw little enough information. If you said to one of them straight, "Is there anything wrong about Wolding?" he would be likely to say something like: "I don't know about anything wrong. We don't go there, that's all."

It isn't that they never discuss queer things; but there is something about the people of Wolding that seems so very queer to them that they don't know where they would get if they once discussed it at all. I doubt if they even think of it.

And then there is the Bishop's influence, spread so widely through his diocese, and always for good, that there is not a calling or occupation in the East Downlands that can be said to be quite unaffected by it. He set that influence from the very first against the Ulford Hounds drawing Wolding, and quiet and restrained though that influence was, it achieved no less

---

[7] A hunting club invented by Dunsany.

success than his more direct commands in the matter of the two summer outings of the Sons of the Church Bicycling Union.

So the world came our way, toward the things that we know today, while Wolding seemed to go by a path of its own, back and back to times that one thought were done with forever. And the more they went backward, the more Nature all round them, with sprouting and singing and prowling, seemed to welcome them on their journey. Young limes seemed to shoot up taller and greener there than they did in the same time elsewhere; dawn seemed to vibrate in Wolding with a denser chorus of blackbirds than in any place that I know; and foxes slipped by at evening near to houses, with a certain air that may have been only my fancy, but that seemed to imply a knowledge that man was coming their way.

At first a few of the bearded Wolding men would come quietly, and even furtively, on market days into Seldham: sugar was one of the things they seemed most to need of the world that lay beyond Wold Hill. But as soon as they had got sufficient beehives they came no longer even for this. Then perhaps no more than two or three times a year a man would slip over the hill to some small town of the downs, to bring back tobacco or to arrange for oranges to be left at a certain point of the Wolding road. The road through Wolding still remained open, if somewhat untidy and narrowed by riotous hedges; but none of those living outside who knew its story came near the place any more, and the few that chanced that way and drove through on some long journey got curious impressions of it that, vague though they were, decided them to go home by some other way.

They had sufficient cattle there, and apples and plenty of pears, some strawberries in their gardens and a profusion of wild ones all over the slopes of the hills, and they cultivated enough crops for their needs, and something more that they stored in their great black barns, built of old beams and flint, and with which they might have bartered had they wished, but they kept themselves to themselves.

Skegland still sold groceries, if he chanced to be in his shop when anyone entered, but he always seemed surprised to see a customer. His supplies grew honester, and safer to eat. After a while he gave up taking money, and merely exchanged what someone wanted for something he wanted himself.

Perkin stayed on, and never left Wolding again. What he had found there it would be hard to say. Evidently content. But as the result of what search or answer the content had come, how could one tell? Those wits were driven too far for us to keep track of them. Of the furthest planets, and the bleak spaces between, and of stars immeasurably beyond our own little group of worlds, he had perpetually sought answers, driven on to question them by a fire in his spirit lit long ago by some grief. To deride him were easy; to keep pace with those wandering wits and say what they sought, and what at last they had found, were a task for some practising philosopher with ample leisure for work. He cut very good hazel-sticks and fastened light axe-heads to them, that he made himself out of flint, and there was scarcely a child in Wolding that had not one of them: indeed those that hadn't an axe of chipped flint had his promise of one before the end of the year.

In Perkin's content Anwrel shared; indeed, after those months of bewilderment and disappointment, he found the restful days that men often look forward to during times of stress, and seldom find, for the world still urges onward though their time of struggle be over; but in Wolding nothing urged onward, and Anwrel found those quiet years of which many dream. To the village he remained the prophet or seer, the first of the men that were as themselves, Tommy Duffin being something apart from all, a being they did not dare to seek to explain. Indeed, Anwrel's weary perplexities being over, there was no one that had any clue to the powers of Tommy Duffin, except old Mrs. Tichener. And she, in her great old age, kept her secret darkly, taking it with her down the declining years, saying nothing of pipes or piper; but everyone saw, even through the veil of her silence, that she treasured a wisdom deeper than all their guesses. Mr. and Mrs. Duffin had no doubt

ch. ends p. 196

more data to go on; but somehow or other had not the knack of putting it all together.

Mrs. End had been right about the children requiring no more arithmetic, and came by much credit for that one remark, for it was of the nature of prophecy. She taught on still at the school, still with the old regularity of certain subjects in certain hours; but the list of a single day taken at random will show how far she had gone with all the rest of them, away from the things that are of importance to us:

9	to	10	snaring.
10	to	11	jam-making.
11	to	12	soaking and cleaning rabbit-skins.
1:30	to	2	chopping.

On other days fishing was taught and every now and then bootmaking.

A longevity came to these people, till it almost seemed as though Death and modern commercialism, in the rush of their work, had forgotten Wolding together; and all the little community seemed surprised when they learned one day that Mrs. Airland was dead. So they put her into the trunk of a hollow tree, which they closed by wrapping it round and round with oziers,[8] and carried her over the hill, and three times round the grave circle of ancient stones; while the pipes of Tommy Duffin uttered what none could say, of their thoughts that hovered reluctant to leave the past, where they crossed and recrossed old memories of Mrs. Airland like butterflies in their play, and then of their guesses peering by few lights into the future, to add their wonder to all that wanders lost in its dusk. And then they buried her just in the edge of the wood, above the field in which those hoary stones had gathered to watch the passing procession of centuries; and tall mysterious foxgloves[9] stood

---

[8] Shoots from a willow tree.

[9] A tall Eurasian plant with erect spikes of thimble-like flowers, typically pinkish-purple or white, shaped like the fingers of gloves.

beside her forever, for the wood was just on the line where the rich clay tips the chalk.

To this queer community recruits came rarely from the lands beyond Wold Hill, from the world and the ways we know; rarely, but yet they came. For those pipes of Tommy Duffin playing often in summer evenings would drift their music perhaps a mile on still air, perhaps much further, till the notes would come to some hill beyond Wolding's woods, where a picnic party from London would be sitting on a Sunday afternoon, throwing broken bottles for fun in the mint and thyme. It had to be a still evening; and even then not a sound would come so far but to ears that, weary with the same old mumble that some machine told over and over and over, were listening for something utterly strange and new. To such ears, as they leaned toward it, that music might faintly reach from where Tommy Duffin played on the slopes of Wolding. After that some girl would slip away alone from the lemonade and gramophone, and was seldom found till long after; and if they ever found her at all she would no longer seem to understand cities. And tired shopwalkers, sick of salesmanship, would sometimes find their way there, pushing through saplings and briar on a Bank-holiday, never to leave the valley for London any more.

One intercourse they had with the outer world; for gypsies came and went by the one road running through Wolding, and camped awhile and passed on again, as though nothing to wonder at had happened at all. These folk soon picked up the knack of bringing whatever the people of Wolding needed from the world that lay over the hill; and any news that ever came into Wolding was always brought by the gypsies. To the tune that Tommy Duffin played on his pipes they would listen gravely and silently, but it never so utterly held them as to keep them forever in Wolding: it seemed rather as though they had some mystery of their own that danced slowly on before them down sunny roads, and that would not abdicate even for the wonder there was in those pipes. Sure of a welcome always, they often came into Wolding, and there the Wolding folk

ch. ends next p.

would gather about them, to hear of the ways of the world they
had forsaken; for, little though any wished to follow those ways,
they found a quaintness in what the world said and did, which
the gypsies never failed to increase in the telling. Thus news
reached Wolding several times in the year, and the cunning
gypsies would get good fruit or corn in exchange.

And though some things altered in Wolding very much,
some altered scarcely at all. To the same eaves the same swallows came on the same date all their lives, a date varying only
a little by our almanacs, and varying not an hour by those
invisible tides on which Spring sails northward in full view of
the swallows. And when Summer ended they twittered and
told the same story, and went the old way. And ploughing
and sowing and harvest all went their round as of old, the
furrows pointing the same way up the field, the sower singing
slowly the same song as he scattered the grain, the harvest
carried in with thankfulness to the unknowable, and all the
old women gleaning. And village festivals, the same year after
year, organised by Anwrel with the assistance of Hibbuts, and
made solemn by the music of Tommy's pipes of reed.

All trivial things, it may be said; unchanging of course, but
too trivial for record. Yet it was amongst such that the people
of Wolding dwelt, and they seemed to find amongst silent
unfoldings and ripenings, that are the great occasions of Nature,
enough to replace those more resounding changes that are the
triumph of man's ingenuity, and which we have gained and
they lost.

HONORARY HEATHEN

The Chagrin of St. Ethelbruda

by S.H. Sime